TROUBLE ON THE
LORDSBURG TRAIL

By the same author

The Man From Shiloh
The Last of the Marauders
The Buffalo Soldier
The Owlhooter
The Cattle Lifters
The Maverick
The Dude
The Pinkerton
The Loner
The Greenhorn
The Gringo General
The Peace Officer
The Chickamaugo Covenant
The Compadres
The Last of the Old Guns
The Beholden Man
A Kansas Bloodletting
The Panhandle Shoot-out
The President's Man
The Law-Bringers

Trouble on the Lordsburg Trail

ELLIOT CONWAY

A Black Horse Western

ROBERT HALE · LONDON

© Elliot Conway 1996
First published in Great Britain 1996

ISBN 0 7090 5690 7

Robert Hale Limited
Clerkenwell House
Clerkenwell Green
London EC1R 0HT

The right of Elliot Conway to be identified as
author of this work has been asserted by him
in accordance with the Copyright, Designs and
Patents Act 1988.

Photoset in North Wales by
Derek Doyle & Associates, Mold, Clwyd.
Printed and bound in Great Britain by
WBC Book Manufacturers Limited,
Bridgend, Mid-Glamorgan.

In memory of Trooper Albert Bunting

ONE

Young Ben Howard caught the tangy smell of wood smoke as he was riding through the shallows of the Hondo, south of Roswell, New Mexico, and made a grab for his Winchester. Then his moment of panic passed and he let the rifle slip back down into its boot.

'Betsy,' he said to his mount, a big mud-coloured, boney-backed mare, 'if it had been Injun campfire smoke, long before I smelt it I'd have been well punctured with feathered sticks and having my hair lifted.'

Coming up the climb from the river bottom-lands Ben saw the fire, set back a piece in a small stand of widely spaced pines away to the right of the trail. He was in need of some chow and coffee not having eaten since sun-up, something like twelve hours ago. Even more than eating he had the urge to pass the time of day with someone more giving to talking than a regular wind-breaking, nine-year-old lump of walking crowbait.

It had been a long and lonely, ball-aching ride from Stillwater Creek on the Canadian in the Nations, Ben thought. The dry, hungry trail across the Texan Panhandle, then drifting south-west towards the Sacramentos and the final stretch of the trail ahead of him to Lordsburg, where his Aunt Vilma lived. Or did the last time his mother had heard from her.

It had been a month since he had seen his ma, after dying from a cancer in her stomach, laid next to Pa's grave. Pa had been dead over two years, having died of gunshot wounds suffered in the line of duty as a law officer. It had been his ma's deathbed wish that had set him on the long ride to Lordsburg. She had made him promise that after she had passed on he would take her jewellery, two rings, a bracelet and a necklace, to her younger sister in Lordsburg as she had no girls of her own to pass them on to. Ben knew that the jewellery couldn't be worth more than a small handful of dollars but a promise was a promise, especially when it was one's own ma's deathbed wish.

There was nothing in Stillwater for him. He couldn't manage the holding on his own and he had no more kin there. M'be he could find some work in Lordsburg helping out on Uncle Joe and Aunt Vilma's ranch. He sold what there was on the holding that the grasping-fingered banker in Sante Fe hadn't claimed, raising enough money to grubstake him and Betsy on the trip to Lordsburg – providing neither of them ate too well or too often.

He had kept clear of any townships along the trail, unless rations were needed for him or Betsy.

Trouble on the Lordsburg Trail 9

There were men there – and women – who, on clapping eyes on him, a young backwoods kid wearing where-they-fitted homespuns, riding a big-footed plough-horse and suspecting that he carried a small roll and some jewellery, would take action to relieve him of them. Ben grinned. The women would m'be be more gentle in cleaning him out but just as efficient, and he would end up as a broke-to-the-wide saddle-bum before he was nineteen.

It was Betsy that had caused him to break the rules of the trail. She had cast a shoe and he was forced to stay on an hour or so while a new shoe was being fitted in a town with the fancy name of Kingsville. There was nothing fancy looking about the outside of the town's only saloon that fronted a mud-slick Main Street he walked into to pass the time away. His ma, Ben thought, had kept her milk cow in a less ramshackle barn. Over the years the scorching winds had made the name of the hotel that had once been painted above the door indecipherable on the sun-bleached planks.

The swing doors squeaked like small vermin in pain and threatened to drop off their hinges as Ben pushed them inwards. The inside of the saloon had the same seedy, time-passed-by look. Two men were standing drinking at the bar and Ben picked out another four customers sitting at a table in a dark corner of the saloon near the rear entrance. He walked over to the bar, the first time he had ever bellied up against one, and, not being a secret drinking man, he shook the lard-faced, thickset barkeep by asking for a soda-pop.

'Soda-pop?' The heavy, hound-like jowls wobbled as the barkeep's jaw dropped open in disbelief.

'Yeah, soda-pop,' repeated Ben. 'Lemonade if you ain't got pop. Something cool being that I'm kinda thirsty.'

'We don't sell that sort of piss in this establishment, bub,' the barkeep said, fish-eyeing him. 'This is a hard-drinkin' man's place.' His fleshy face loosened further in a sneering mocking grin. 'M'be I could rustle up a glass of milk for you, if you don't mind the glass being dirty.'

Ben's face reddened in anger and embarrassment. He was about to tell the fat slob of a barkeep that his place wasn't clean enough to keep hogs in let alone serve drinks in when one of the two drinkers at the bar sidled up to him, a big, black-whiskered man who towered over him. The big man placed a bottle of whiskey on the bar next to Ben's right hand. Grinning a gap-toothed, mirthless smirk he said, 'Yuh take a pull or two of that grow'd up liquor, boy, and be sociable. Yuh can't come ridin' into our town and give Jake there a heart attack by askin' him tuh serve yuh a namby-pamby drink like soda-pop. M'be when yuh've downed half the bottle it'll warm yur blood up, give yuh a hankerin' to take Lucy, standin' by the boys there, upstairs.' The mocking leer broadened. 'She'll show yuh how tuh go on if yuh ain't sampled what she offers before.'

Ben shot a squint-eyed look at Lucy. She looked

Trouble on the Lordsburg Trail

as old as his ma the day she died yet she had a dress on as short as a twelve-year-old girl would wear – and as pretty-faced as the hairy gorilla who was crowding him. He had no burning urge to go upstairs with Lucy to partake in what she offered, drunk or stone-cold sober. Nervously he ran his tongue over dry lips. He was no bigger coward than the next man facing a tricky situation that could turn into a violent confrontation.

A man of his own weight and height, m'be even a few pounds heavier, he would have had no hesitation in tackling. But to wrestle for real with the big man was asking for several of his bones being broken. Ben bit the bullet. The trouble wasn't going to blow over, the big man was pushing it to a fight. He would be damned if he was going to let him rub his nose in the shit. He remembered his pa telling him that he hadn't to wait till any trouble coming his way overwhelmed him.

'Meet it halfway, boy,' he had said. 'Don't let whoever's proddin' you dictate all the moves. Catch him off balance by taking the fight to him.'

'Get drinkin', asshole,' the big man snarled. 'Lucy's gettin' herself all worked up waitin' for yuh.' A big ham of a hand's fingers dug viciously into Ben's left shoulder, causing him to wince with pain. The trouble the big bastard was siccing on him had definitely gone over the halfway mark. It was time either to eat crow or do what his pa had said. And Ben didn't lack the grit to fight back.

He snatched up the whiskey bottle and with a backhanded, swinging swipe, landed the bottle on the big man's temple, with such force that it knocked him heavily to the floor without even a whisper of a groan, out to the wide. Ben whirled round from the bar, still gripping the bottle, and faced the drinkers at the tables. White-faced, eyes mad-glaring, he yelled, 'You saw the sonuvabitch hazzlin' me! He was out to make trouble for me for no damn reason at all! Any of you gents thinking the same way?' Ben waved the bottle threateningly and waited for a moment or two to see if any of them were going to take up from where the man lying at his feet had been cut off. Seeing no aggressive movement from any of the card players Ben turned back to mean-eye the barkeep.

'It ain't exactly a *welcome stranger* gin mill you're running here, mister, is it?' he grated, then placed the bottle on the bar with trembling hands before walking across to the door, having to force his equally shaking legs to make the necessary movements, hoping that the smith had finished shoeing Betsy. He had a burning urge now to put as much territory between him and Kingsville before the big man came to.

The short-time girl's shout of, 'Look-out kid!', and the sound of the pistol shot, its load ripping through the door in front of his face, sounding simultaneously, Ben spun round on his heels in alarm and saw the big man's drinking partner aiming a pistol at him for a second shot. The .36 Colt, his pa's old pistol, seemed to jump into his

Trouble on the Lordsburg Trail

hand from the waistband of his pants and fire one shot on its own accord, as though his dead pa was handling it. And his pa had taught him well in the drawing, aiming and firing of a pistol. 'Don't aim to wing a man who has thrown down on you, he's trying to kill you; you do likewise. Make it a head shot,' had been his expert advice.

Ben's snap-shot put a neat black, red-tinged hole in the middle of the gunman's forehead, its exit much messier, blowing away most of the back of his head. The impact of the shell flung him back against the bar, his pistol, triggered by dying reflexes, discharged its load harmlessly into the ceiling as he slid to the floor, to fall across his still unconscious pard, never to come to this side of the gates of hell.

Ben stood at the door, half crouched, face frozen in a cornered wolf-like grimace of defiance. A man got up from one of the tables and walked towards him. Ben swung his gun round and covered him. The man stopped and raised both hands, palms outwards and Ben saw the glint of a lawman's badge pinned to his vest.

'Easy kid,' the lawman said. 'I'm Sheriff Rodgers, reckon to uphold the law hereabouts. I saw that you were drawn on first and there ain't no case can be made against a man who plugs a sneaky, no-good, backshooting sonuvabitch so you can put your hogleg away.'

Miller dead was no loss to the community. Rodgers wouldn't have shed any tears if Bully Hogan had been sent to where Miller was now instead of just being laid out cold. Even if the pair of them had been upright, law-abiding citizens he wouldn't have run the kid in.

The territory was crawling with itchy-triggered youngsters building themselves reps as *pistoleros*. The baby-cheeked bastards were lifting cattle, shooting dead anyone who tried to stop them, lawmen, cowhands or whoever. With as much remorse in their black souls as though it was a make-believe kids' game they were playing. Some of them, Billy Bonney, Dick Brewer, Bill McNab and a few other like-minded youngsters, calling themselves The Boys, had a small war going full blast around the county seat.

The speed this kid had pulled out his gun and plumb shot Miller dead he could be one of the Bonney gang and if he jailed him The Boys could stop their rustling of John Chisum's cattle and come ass-kicking it into Kingsville and shoot his ears off and spring the kid from his cell. No sir, Sheriff Rodgers silently decided, he wasn't about to invite the wild boys to pay him a visit, bringing all the shooting and killing to his town. He smiled fatherly at Ben. 'Though I'd better warn you to leave town, *pronto*, kid,' he said. 'Or you'll have some more shootin' to do. Bully Hogan won't take it kindly you cold-cockin' him. And he'll be no less happier when he finds out you've shot dead his drinking pardner.'

Ben took another fascinated, horrified look at the man he had killed before saying, 'I was just about to do that, Sheriff, only that fella,' he

Trouble on the Lordsburg Trail

pointed his pistol at the dead man, 'thought he had the God-given right to stop me.' He eased the hammer of his pistol forward and stuffed it back down the top of pants. 'I'll leave town as soon as I collect my horse from the stable, Sheriff.' Raising his hat to Lucy he said, 'Thanks for your warning, ma'am. At least you've been friendly.' He took a final look at the two bodies before turning and walking out of the saloon, his yearning for a glass of soda-pop completely gone.

Ben stopped at the entrance of the first alley he came to and threw up. His pa might have taught him to shoot fast and accurately but he hadn't been able to teach him how he should control his reactions after killing a man for the first time. Yet killing men in the line of duty hadn't seemed to have affected his pa in any way. Leastways his pa hadn't let any upset show if it had. Like everything else, Ben thought morbidly, shooting men dead would be only a matter of getting used to. Though it was a chore he fervently hoped he wouldn't get too familiar with. Getting used to it or not, he'd be damned if he was going to let any prodding asshole shoot him down like a dog. His pa hadn't raised a chicken-livered turn-tail.

Once clear of Kingsville Ben began to ride through bunches of cattle as thick, he thought, as once the buffalo must have been when sighted by the first plainsmen. He saw distant columns of smoke, cow-camp smoke, but kept to the main trail. He hadn't raised enough dust between him and Kingsville to stop him from peering over his shoulder to see if a black-whiskered rider was pounding along his back-trail.

Ben drew up just short of the trees and hulloed the camp, a one-man camp. A man with a horse and a pack-mule, making him think that the man was a trader of some sort. 'Is it OK if I come on in, mister, and use your fire to warm up some beans?' he called out.

The man at the fire waved a come-on-in-hand and shouted, 'You're welcome to step down, pilgrim. And there ain't no need for you to open a can of beans. There's plenty of wind-breakers in the pan if you ain't fussy about sharin' another wanderer's leavin's.'

Ben let Betsy pick her own way through the trees towards the camp then dismounted. He stepped the few paces to the fire and looked down at the Good Samaritan sitting there. He grinned. 'Friend, I ain't much of a hand in fixin' beans, or any other vittals for that matter, so once I've seen to my horse I'll gladly partake in sharing your beans.'

While eating his beans Ben took a closer look at the man whose food and coffee he was enjoying. He was white-haired, worn long in plainsman fashion, with a face as weathered and creased as the buffalo-hide coat he had slung over his shoulders. By the smell coming from it Ben thought unkindly, half of the buffalo must still be inside it. There was nothing weathered or old about the needle-sharp blue eyes that were doing some assessing of their own.

Respecting the protocol of chance meetings on the trail each waited for the other to volunteer the information of who they were and where they were bound for. Ben could see several skins, coyotes, wolves, hanging from nearby branches so he opined that the old man was not a trader but was working for some rancher, being paid a bounty for every dead calf-killer he brought in. He also thought, being that the old man had shared his camp and food with him, it was only right and proper for him to be just as sociable by telling who he was and where he was heading for, first.

'Howard, you say, from way up in the Nations,' the old hunter said after hearing Ben out. He ruminated for a while before saying, 'I heard of a Howard lawman, working out of Fort Smith, Arkansas. Saw him ride into Fort Smith leadin' the Bolton cousins, all three of 'em, wrapped up neat and tidy-like in their waterproofs across their horses, neat and tidy dead. The way Marshal Howard looked it didn't seem long before he would be lying as stiff and dead as the cousins. I heard later that he was carrying several pieces of the wild boys' lead in him. Was he any kin of yours?'

Ben's face coloured with pride. 'He was my pa.'

The old hunter's face cracked open in a smile. 'Well, well, well, ain't it a small world? Is your pa still roundin' up hard-cases for Judge Parker?'

Ben shook his head 'No, he's been dead over a year now. You had heard right about him being wounded, he never rode out again for the judge.

The gunshots turned bad on him and he died hard and painfully. Then my ma was took from me. It's her last wish that's got me on the trail to Lordsburg.'

'I'm right sorry to hear about your losses, kid. Your pa was a good lawman, hard but fair. My handle is Matt Forest, earn my beans and coffee by killin' the varmints that pester Mr Chisum's cattle.' His face crinkled up again in a smile. 'The four-legged variety that is. The two-legged I leave to the lawmen to dispose of.'

Ben was finishing off the last of his beans when he saw five slow-riding horsemen closing in on the camp. Wary-eyed he put his plate down and rested a hand on the butt of his pistol. It could be Bully Hogan with a few of his friends riding in to even up the score he thought grimly. Matt Forest saw the move and opined that somewhere behind him the kid had stirred up trouble for himself which, he thought, wasn't surprising. Right now the territory was knee-deep in trouble. He only hoped that the kid hadn't brought some of it up to his campfire. His kindness could be responsible for getting him killed.

Matt Forest's, 'Well I'll be durned, it's Mr John Chisum himself,' as he got to his feet eased Ben's fears and his hand fell away from the pistol as he stood up alongside the old hunter.

'You musta ridden through some of his longhorns, Mr Howard, once you crossed the Pegos,' Matt Forest said. 'He owns over ten thousand of them. Yet he don't like losin' as much

Trouble on the Lordsburg Trail 19

as one maverick unnatural-like. There's a bunch of wild boys, not much older than you, liftin' his cattle. Selling them, so talk has it, to Brad Logan who ranches south of here, White Sands way. He aims to run as many cattle as Chisum and ain't fussy whose beef he takes to do it. The tall *hombre* ridin' alongside Chisum is Pat F. Garrett, the Lincoln lawman, Chisum's man. Paid to put an end to the cattle-lifting.'

Ben took in the two big store-suited men, Pat Garrett towering well over six feet, both men favouring black longhorn moustaches. Indian-faced they both subjected Ben to a hard-eyed, weighing-up stare. The other men, shut-faced individuals who, Ben reckoned, were Garrett's deputies, were casting him the same unfriendly looks.

Matt Forrest laughed. 'There ain't no need to give the kid fish-eyed looks, he ain't one of Billy the Kid's gang. He's trailed here from the Nations, headin' to see his kin in Lordsburg. His pa was a marshal, Pat, name of Sam Howard. Kept the peace in the territory for Judge Parker.'

'I've heard of him,' Pat Garrett said. 'First-class thief-taker by all accounts, and one of the fastest men with a pistol around.'

Garrett's statement eased the tension and the riders relaxed back in their saddles.

'If you care to step down, gents, I'll get some coffee brewin',' Matt Forest said then he grinned. 'It's open-house today.'

Over coffee Ben heard for the first time of Billy

the Kid and his gang of youthful desperadoes and their part in the Lincoln County war. 'Mr Chisum and me, and everyone else in the county for that matter, know that Billy is taking his cattle and selling them to Brad Logan but we can't get enough proof of the illegal deals to stand up in a court of law. The war's split the county into two factions. Billy has a lot of friends and they will swear on a stack of Bibles that Billy was whoopin' it up in some *cantina* below the line when the cattle was being lifted.'

'We think that we've got a break now though,' John Chisum broke in, taking over the story. 'A Mr Lou Stoker, who farms near Tularosa, wrote to me saying that he's willing to stand up in front of a judge and jury and give dates, and the numbers of cattle stamped with the Jingle-Bob brand – my mark – William Bonney handed over to Logan's straw boss. Seemingly, according to his letter, Logan welshed on some payment he owed him. My feeling is that Stoker played some part in the cattle deals. Probably let them use his land to move the stolen cattle across till Logan got them rebranded. But that's neither here or there. Putting an end to my cattle being lifted is all that matters. I'm on my way to see Mr Stoker now. Sheriff Garrett and his deputies are riding with me to make sure that no harm befalls Stoker till he testifies. The law down there favours Mr Logan's interests.'

John Chisum tossed the dregs of his coffee on to the ashes then looked across at Ben.

'If you're ready to move out, Mr Howard,' he said, 'you're welcome to ride with us as far as Tularosa. Coming in we picked up sign of five, six horses, unshod mounts, bare-assed riders with feathers in their hair and blood hate in their hearts, no doubt sitting up on their backs. Meet up with them and you'll never make Lordsburg.' He thin-smiled at Matt Forest. 'You should be OK, Mr Forest, the tracks led south.'

The old trapper swore loudly and shot an angry scowling look at Pat Garrett. 'What with all the shootin' goin' on between The Boys and the so-called law around here and now a bunch of reservation-jumpin', hair-liftin' bucks roamin' around the territory it ain't safe for an old man to be out tryin' to earn his livin'.'

Pat Garrett grinned. 'You just pull up stakes and head north to Lincoln you'll be OK. No Injun will jump you, they'll not be able to stand the smell.'

Matt Forest cut loose with another string of curses then got to his feet and began cutting down the pelts from the trees. Ben stood up and prepared Betsy for the journey south. Bad white men, now bad Indians, he thought gloomily. He knew that the ride to Lordsburg wouldn't be like some quiet stroll down a back-country turnpike but neither did he think that he would have to use his pistol and kill to defend himself.

TWO

Jos Spicer, Brad Logan's straw boss, walked into the big house without first knocking at the front door and allowing the rancher's Mexican housekeeper, to open the door and formally lead him to his employer's den.

Logan, sitting at his desk working on his tally books, pleased with the speed his herd was being built up, looked up in surprise at the unexpected appearance of his foreman.

'I thought you were in Tularosa, Spicer,' he said. 'Drinking in the Bull's Head.'

'So I was boss,' replied Spicer. 'Till Stoker started shoutin' his mouth out. Tellin' all within hearing distance how he's goin' to put paid to that asshole – his word not mine, boss – who fancies himself as King of Tularosa by tellin' Mr John Chisum about the fella who's stealin' his cattle and in whose hands they end up in. He also blabbed about Chisum comin' to Tularosa to see him. I thought you oughta know about his blabbin' *pronto*, boss. You could be in real trouble especially if Chisum brings his hired lawman, Pat Garrett and his deputies with him.'

Trouble on the Lordsburg Trail 23

And for him, thought Spicer. If Chisum got proof that his boss was knowingly buying his stolen cattle Chisum would hang every cowhand on Logan's payroll. As he would be entitled to being that it was plainsfolk law that cattle and horse-thieves could be shot dead on sight or summarily hanged.

'Why the loose-lipped sonuvabitch,' Logan breathed softly but vehemently. 'He would have gone to the wall long since if I hadn't paid him hard cash to look the other way when Billy the Kid was driving Chisum's beef over his land. He's been trying to squeeze more cash out of me but I turned him down. I reckon that's why he's going to talk to Chisum. That bastard will pay plenty to bring me down. Then he'll have all the grass from here to Lincoln for his cattle to chew on.'

Logan eased his great bulk in his seat and his eyes closed momentarily in concentration. He hadn't got to be a serious challenger to John Chisum as the biggest rancher in New Mexico by spending sleepless nights biting his fingernails trying to resolve burning issues or problems. His overweight may have made him a slow ponderous walker, even forcing him to have a hand-up to get astride his horse, but his brain wasn't sluggish moving. He was capable of assessing any situation facing him, however black-looking, and come up with a face-saving solution as quick as a tinhorn would declare his bid.

What helped Logan's quick decision-making was that he didn't give a damn if people got stomped on, if that was required, in overcoming any obstacle in his way to the top. He opened his eyes and gave Spicer a beady-eyed look. 'Get hold of Kerney, Spicer. I reckon the horn dog will be in the Sporting House. Get his ass out here, *pronto*, even if you have to interrupt his pleasuring. No, wait, get my horse saddled up, I'll ride with you as far as Sandy Creek, bring him there, it'll save a little time. We don't know how close Chisum is to Tularosa.'

Kerney looked every inch the cold-blooded cut-throat that people who had never seen a killer before would imagine how such a man would look. He wasn't a big-framed man but his unblinking snake-eyed, all bone-face would deter many a heftier man from pressing any disagreement he may have with Kerney to the full, backing off, willing to eat crow, before it came to the point where only drawn pistols would settle the argument. Unless the man was hankering to fill a plot in Boot Hill.

Kerney's face was no more human-looking for having been literally dragged off his favourite whore in the Sporting House, a hot-assed redhead, by Spicer. He pulled up his horse and swung out of his saddle and walked along the creek bank to meet up with Logan. It was in the fat man's favour that he paid well for his services rendered or he would have told Spicer to tell his boss to go to hell. Kerney cold-smiled. Being well paid or not if he had actually been performing

Trouble on the Lordsburg Trail

with the redhead he would have plugged Spicer well and truly dead for putting him off his stride.

Logan, cigar clamped between his teeth, stood with his back to the creek equally flint-eyeing Kerney as he came towards him. Kerney had helped him out several times, putting the fear of the Almighty into small ranchers reluctant to leave their land when offered what he considered a fair price for it so that he could have the extra grass and water for his growing herds. The real stubborn ranchers, men who had wrested their sections of land from the Indians and the Mexicans and felt that they had earned the right to hold on to it, come hell and high water, ended up shot dead by bushwhackers, as yet unknown, as the coroner's juries put it. Kerney also supplied him with a steady stream of longhorns lifted from border ranches in Arizona. All in all a good man to have on hand.

Kerney's way of earning a living, though up till now the law couldn't prove that he was a cattle-thief and a killer, meant that outwardly law-abiding, respectable citizens, up-and coming big men in the territory couldn't be seen to be even drinking in the same bar as him. Not if they wanted to progress further up the social and political ladder in the territory.

Both men nodded curtly to each other then, being individuals who thought along the same no-nonsense violent lines, Logan didn't waste time pussy-footing talking around the reason of his wanting to see Kerney urgently.

'I want Lou Stoker silenced, for keeps,' he said. 'If you don't know him by sight, Spicer will point him out to you.'

'When do you want this to happen, Mr Logan?' Kerney asked.

'Like as now,' the rancher snapped back. 'He's stirring up big trouble for me.'

What that trouble was didn't concern Kerney. Just the payment mattered. He bared his teeth in a mirthless grin. 'No problem, Mr Logan. The sonuvabitch is already dead but he don't know it yet. You just get Spicer to finger him, that's all.'

Logan nodded his head in satisfaction. One problem sorted out, he turned and looked across the creek. 'There's another job, a big one if you want it, Kerney,' he said.

'As long as the money's big I'm interested, Mr Logan,' replied Kerney.

Logan swung his gaze back on to the gunman again. 'John Chisum is expected in Tularosa at any time,' he said. 'Marshal Pat Garrett could be riding with him. If Chisum could meet up with a fatal shooting accident on the trail before he reaches Tularosa I'd make the payment big enough. And I could up the price if Garrett happened to get caught up in the same accident.'

Kerney let out his breath in a long, low whistle. 'Mr Logan,' he said admiringly, 'I know now why they call you King of Tularosa.' He could have told the rancher that he knew of a man who would walk barefooted across red-hot embers to get a clear shot at Chisum and Garrett, all for free, but

Trouble on the Lordsburg Trail 27

a man has to earn his living. He favoured the rancher with another wolf-like smile. 'Mr Logan, you buy yourself a wreath; you'll be attendin' the biggest funeral the territory's seen in a few days' time.'

'Good,' replied Logan and handed Kerney a thick roll of dollar bills. He smiled, a forked-tongued, skin-deep exercise. 'There'll be as much again when I hear of Chisum's and Garrett's deaths. I think you'll agree that it's more than a fair price for the chore.'

It was a real fair price for Logan; he had no intention of handing over the second half of the due. Normally Spicer acted as his go-between with Kerney, relaying any orders he had for him by meeting up with the gunman in some bar or whorehouse in Tularosa, enabling him to keep a respectable distance between him and a man who, all things being equal, should have been strung up a long time ago.

The killing of Chisum and Garrett would set the territory buzzing like an upturned hornets' nest. Though the Murphy and Dolan faction in Lincoln were known enemies of Chisum the finger of suspicion could also be pointed at him. The whole cattle trade knew that he hankered after wearing Chisum's crown so the fewer who knew about his latest deal with Kerney the easier he could ride out any shit that came his way.

As far as Spicer knew all he wanted Kerney for was to put paid to a ragged-assed sodbuster; Spicer, being a cattleman, who hated sodbusters for destroying fine grass, would go along with the killing. Most likely the shooting of Garrett wouldn't upset him too much. Men like Spicer had upheld the law west of the Pegos by the speedy justice of the Colt, the Winchester and the hanging tree. They didn't take kindly to official lawmen who opined that men who broke the cattleman's law deserved a fair and just trial. Killing Chisum, another cattleman, could strain Spicer's loyalty to him. To protect his ass Kerney would have to die. The next time he came riding across Bar X land he would see to it that the son-of-a-bitch was shot down like the cattle-thief he was. Then only he would know who gave the orders to kill Chisum and Garrett, leaving his image as an up-and-coming cattle baron untarnished. After Kerney had left, Logan walked across to his horse so well pleased with his plan and the goal it would achieve for him he managed to clamber up into his saddle unaided.

Once back in Tularosa Kerney toured the bars and saloons and rousted out Doroleo Pena, his right-hand man in the small band of like-minded back-shooters and cattle-lifters he bossed over. Pena was part-Mexican, part-Indian but, like Kerney, a full-blood killer. On the boardwalk, well away from the saloon section of Main Street and the bustle of men seeking their pleasures, Kerney told the breed of the business in hand for the Kerney gang.

'The man who's payin' us to silence Stoker,' he

Trouble on the Lordsburg Trail

said, 'is also payin' us a lot extra for seeing John Chisum, and that bastard Garrett, if he's with him, planted. The big cattleman is due in town soon.' Kerney cold-smiled as he saw Pena's normally expressionless face light up. 'I thought that you'd be more than a mite interested bein' that Chisum strung your brother up for stealin' a few of his lousy cows, and him havin' to be roped to his horse under the hangin' tree on account he'd been all shot to hell by Pat Garrett. I reckon that you and two of the boys should get the drop on those two bastards between here and where they are on the trail. If Garrett has deputies with him don't take 'em on. We ain't getting paid to fight a small war. We'll just have to sneak up on the pair of them when they come riding into Tularosa. I'll stay and see that the sodbuster, Stoker stops his blabbing, for keeps.'

Pena gave Kerney another surprise, by smiling albeit without an ounce of good-natured feeling in it. 'Killing Chisum and Garrett will give me greater pleasure than humping a woman. I'll take Leroy and Shorty with me. We'll ride out at once.'

'*Bueno, amigo,*' said Kerney. 'Good huntin'.'

Kerney waited in the darkness of the store porch till Pena came out of the Bull's Head again with Leroy and Shorty in tow. He grinned thinly. He knew the pair would not be too happy being dragged away from the women and the liquor. But what the hell, he thought, the business they were in didn't have regular hours like some store clerk's job. He watched them ride out of town before making contact with Logan's straw boss. It didn't do to let any of his gang know who the man was who was paying them to do the killings. One of them might get the fancy notion of going into business on his own and offer the same service for less payment. Money in the hand and looking out for number one came well ahead of loyalty to his buddies in the Kerney gang.

An hour later Kerney was standing with his back up against the inside wall of the White Sands saloon, idly drawing on a makings, but keen-eyeing the small, narrow-shouldered man's tangle-footed progress towards the door. Kerney's lips drew back in a grimace of well-being. It would be like money from home putting paid to Stoker. The sodbuster was too drunk to put up any sort of a struggle. He would be dead before he cottoned on to the fact that he had been knifed.

Casually he followed Stoker out of the saloon and dogged him till he stepped off the boardwalk to stumble across the mouth of a dark alley. It was quiet and dark enough so Kerney quickly decided to earn Logan's first payment. He closed up on Stoker and wrapped his left arm around his neck, choking off his feeble protests as he bundled him into the alley. Once clear of the street he thrust the knife, held in his right hand deep into Stoker's side. Stoker felt a split-second of coldness in his stomach as the blade sank into his flesh then a burning sensation that reached right up to the back of his throat. His dying scream came out as a muffled gurgle as his mouth filled with blood. Kerney held on to him for the few moments it took him to die. He dragged the body deeper into the alley before pulling out the knife and wiping it clean on Stoker's shirt. A real grin came on to Kerney's face. As he had thought earlier on, it was like money from home. If Pena and the boys had the same sort of luck the Kerney gang looked like being real high-rollers for quite a while to come. To pass away the time till Pena came back with the good news he would pay a visit to the redhead, m'be stir her blood up some more by promising to buy her a new dress.

Within easy riding distance of Tularosa Pat Garrett drew up his horse and suggested to Mr Chisum that they make camp. 'I'll send my deputies into Tularosa in the morning to find out where this fella Stoker's land is, discreetly like of course. Me and you are too well known to ride into the place and openly ask about the whereabouts of Stoker. Logan's men will be drinking in town and if they get wind of our enquiries they'll pass the news on to their boss and Stoker's life will be on the line.'

'That makes sense, Pat,' Mr Chisum said. He smiled. 'Though I'm not looking forward to another cold and hard-on-the-bones night camp.'

Pat Garrett smiled back. 'None of us is getting any younger Mr Chisum.' He turned to face Ben. 'Are you riding into Tularosa, Mr Howard, to spend a comfortable night under a roof, sitting at a table to eat your chow?'

'No, Mr Garrett,' replied Ben. 'I've got to make my cash stretch as far as Lordsburg.' His face darkened. 'And besides the last town I visited only got me into a heap of trouble,' Ben looked at Garrett full in the eyes. 'Though not of my making, Mr Garrett.'

Pat Garrett had ceased to wonder what sort of trouble baby-faced kids could land themselves in. The smooth-faced kids were good at making their own brand of trouble. Billy the Kid and his boys were giving him and other law-enforcers a whole bellyful of rustling and killing trouble.

'You're welcome to share our camp, Mr Howard,' John Chisum said. 'There's no sense you riding off and setting up a camp on your own.'

'Thanks, Mr Chisum,' said Ben. 'I'd appreciate that. As I said to Mr Forest, fixin' chow ain't one of my better chores.'

THREE

Pena believed that the saints had smiled on him as he saw the three men mount up and leave the camp in the direction of Tularosa. He and the boys had come on Chisum's camp less than an hour's ride from town. Dismounting and Indian-in closer he opined, by the unreliable light from the fire, there were at least six men in the camp. Disappointedly he couldn't tell which of them was Chisum and Garrett. Kerney had told him to avoid a small gun battle and that's what it would turn into if he cut loose at the camp now. They could, even in the bad light, drop three of them, but with no guarantee that any of the three would be Chisum or Garrett. The rest would scatter among the brush and the rocks, and being hard-assed men they'd take them on at even odds. Odds Pena didn't fancy.

'We'll pull back behind the last ridge we crossed, bed down for the night there,' he had said. Then a little after sun-up they had closed in on Chisum's camp again, this time on foot, and just in time to see the deputies ride out, leaving, as he could clearly see, Chisum, Garrett and a young kid at the camp. Pena decided, now the luck seemed to be coming his way, instead of picking off his intended targets by rifle fire from the high ground he and his boys would sneak up on the camp and get the drop on the three of them then he would have the greater pleasure of slipping a rope round Chisum's and Garrett's necks. Set them dancing on air as the bastards did to his brother. He would simply plug the kid having no special grievance against him.

Ben had saddled-up Betsy, strapped on his bedroll, seen to it that his canteen was full, then climbed out of the shallow basin where the horses had been tethered for the night and walked back to the camp to say his goodbyes to his trail companions. Suddenly a man stepped out from the brush to his left and jabbed a rifle into his back.

'You just keep on strolling to the camp, kid,' Shorty said. 'Give me as much as an unkind look and I'll blow your backbone clear through your chest, and that's a fact, kid.'

Ben gave the man a slant-eyed look then with his right hand, slowly and unobtrusively he buttoned up his jacket to cover the butt of the Navy jutting above the top of his pants, not doubting that any seen move would get him killed. As he walked towards the fire he saw that Mr Chisum and Mr Garrett were in the same situation as he was, covered by rifles held by two more men.

Pena quickly looked Ben over and saw a

Trouble on the Lordsburg Trail 35

scared-looking unarmed *gringo* kid, quickly dismissing him as a possible danger to the edge he had over Chisum and Garrett. 'You move over to the other two, kid,' he said. He allowed himself a slight smile of accomplishment. Like Kerney he felt that it was going to be money easy earned.

'The boy has no part in this,' Chisum said. 'We only picked him up along the trail. Let him ride out.'

'Too late for that, Señor Chisum,' Pena said. He grinned mockingly at the rancher. 'I can't have the kid going to the law saying that he can describe the likeness of the *hombres* who strung up Señor "Big Hombre" Chisum and his paid marshal, Señor Garrett, can I?' Pena saw Garrett stiffen and eye the rifle resting on a rock by the fire. 'You'll never make it, Garrett, unless you favour dying by the bullet instead of the rope. Even then you'll not succeed because I'll only wing you. Then you'll feel like my brother felt when you hung him from a tree after you'd gunshot him real bad. Just for lifting a few of your cows, Señor Chisum.'

'I opine that you must be another Pena,' Chisum said. 'You have the same mean-faced bushwhacking look, too yellow to face a man on level terms in the open. Your brother back-shot two of my linemen; I hanged him for that, not for being a no-good, sonuvabitch cattle-thief. Though to be truthful if I could have hanged him twice he would have swung for rustling as well.'

Pena's rifle shook in his hands. Face working in

mad-assed rage he snarled at Shorty: 'Get their horses up here, *pronto*, and we'll have us a hanging party. I reckon you ought to know, Señor Chisum, being that it's too late for you to do anything about it, someone else would like to see you dead. Paying good money to us to make it so.'

Strung up by murderous assholes, Ben thought angrily, though cold logic prevented him from yanking out his pistol in a forlorn hope of getting Pena before the sure fact that the other gunman would kill him dead. Always play it cool had been his pa's advice. Play for time if you've been boxed in so that you can come up with a move that can shorten the odds against you. Remember, he had added, you're not dead till you've ceased to breathe.

Getting some sort of an advantage over Pena and his pard wasn't going to be easy. They weren't drunken blowhards like the two in the saloon. They were hired guns, professional killers; eyes-in-their-asses men. One thing was for sure, whatever he had to do to try and save himself and his two trail companions from being lynched had to be done now. When the odds were only two to one. In spite of the hairy situation he was in Ben smiled inwardly. His pa would have thought that the odds favoured him.

Pena, at least, would have to be distracted long enough for Ben to reach under his coat and pull off a shot. He caught Mr Chisum's eye and gave him a slight nod and hoped that the rancher would get the message that things were about to happen.

Trouble on the Lordsburg Trail 37

At first Chisum was puzzled by Ben's signal. How the hell could an unarmed kid get the better of two *pistoleros*, he thought. Then he remembered that Mr Howard carried a gun in the top of his pants. Even so the kid was taking a big chance to save them all from a hanging. But, Chisum soberly opined, whatever the kid was about to try it was their only hope of salvation. He didn't believe in divine miracles happening. Not to big sinners like him anyways. He gave an answering nod back and waited.

Although expecting Ben's move, Chisum was surprised how he played it. Ben half turned from the two gunmen and holding his stomach began retching as though about to throw-up. Pena swung his rifle on to him then started to grin. 'What's up, kid, ain't taken part in a hanging before?' He brought the rifle back on to Chisum and Garrett.

Ben winked at Chisum and the rancher got the drift of Ben's ploy. The kid had fooled Pena into thinking that there was no need for an eagle eye on a seemingly shit-scared kid. Now, he reckoned, it was up to him to see to it that the Mexican's attention was kept away from the kid.

'You can see the boy's scared to death, Pena,' he said. 'Let us all go and whatever amount you've been paid to kill us, I'll double it, in gold. And you'll have my word that the law won't hunt you and your men down. It will be strictly a business deal.'

Pena's mercenary mind began to work overtime

at the mention of gold. He close-eyed Chisum as he weighed up his options. Avenging the death of his brother didn't enter into his thinking at all. His thought was how a deal with Chisum would make him rich, enabling him to pleasure prettier city women, down fine city liquor. Kiss dog-shit towns like Tularosa goodbye. If Chisum had strung up the whole of his family it wouldn't have stopped him from taking up Chisum's offer and high-tailing it for the big times. But taking Chisum's money meant crossing Kerney, and that sonuvabitch was one mean *hombre*. He would track him down, right to the Canadian border, if needs be, as a matter of principle to kill him.

Before he could refuse Chisum's offer, Ben, still bent low, fired from beneath his coat, the muzzle-flash searing a smouldering, flame-tinged hole in the cloth. Pena staggered back several places as though buffeted by a strong wind as the shell caught him full in the face turning it into a bloody, shapeless mess, killing him dead in an instant of time. Ben didn't see him fall to the ground, he had his pistol clear of his coat triggering off a second snap-shot at the other hired gun. Another killing shot sent the man spinning round on his heels then folding in the middle as he collapsed to the ground. Garrett sprang forward and grabbed hold of his rifle. Hip-high he began pumping out loads at Shorty.

Shorty, halfway between the hollow and the camp had never seen a situation change so quickly. The downing of Pena and Leroy had

Trouble on the Lordsburg Trail 39

happened so fast he could hardly take it in. The Winchester shells hissing ominously close to him underlined what he had seen was for real. He was on his own. It was, he quickly opined, cut-and-run time, unless he wanted to meet up with Pena and Leroy in hell or wherever. He jumped astride the only horse of the three he was leading that was saddled-up, an old wall-eyed grey that looked more like a plough-horse than a saddle-horse. But there was no time to pick and choose, as Shorty knew, any four-legged critter can run faster than a man. Crouching low across the saddle he savagely rib-kicked the mare back the way he had led it. He gave a yelp of pain and his right ear stung like a whiplash burn and he sensed the sticky warmth of blood running down his cheek, then he was in the hollow out of sight of Garrett and his Winchester.

'The sonuvabitch has taken Betsy!' Ben yelled. Frustratedly he fired the remaining loads in the Colt at the spot Shorty had dipped down into the hollow.

John Chisum dabbed at his face and neck with a handkerchief with a hand that shook slightly. Not only was he getting too old for cold night camps, he thought sourly, he was definitely getting too damned ancient to spit in the eye of Death. Chisum looked at Ben. The kid seemed almost in tears. He had gunned down two *pistoleros* who had the drop on him without turning a hair yet he was getting all worked-up over losing a field-horse. 'Don't fret none about losing your horse, Mr

Howard,' he said. 'I'll be pleased to buy you a whole remuda when we get to Tularosa. You've sure earned a string of horses.'

'It ain't that the sonuvabitch just took Betsy, Mr Chisum,' Ben said. 'He's taken the jewellery that was in my saddle-bags.'

'Jewellery?' said Mr Chisum. He shot a puzzled glance at Pat Garrett who had joined them after professionally inspecting the two outlaws to check out that they had ceased being a threat to them.

Garrett wasn't as puzzled as Mr Chisum on hearing Ben mention jewllery. Kids his age were holding up stages, robbing banks, lifting cattle. Anything the wrong side of the law to earn their living. Making their hard-working fathers wonder what sort of kids they had sired. Mr Howard could just be following the trend the young-bloods were setting in present-day New Mexico. He had spoken of getting into trouble some place or other. It could have been when he came by the jewels. Though the kid had said that the trouble hadn't been of his making. But Billy the Kid could lie through his back teeth, Garrett thought, and smile like a saint while he was doing it. 'Were the jewels valuable, Mr Howard?' he asked probingly.

'I don't reckon so, Mr Garrett,' replied Ben. 'But that ain't the point, they belonged to my ma.' He then told Garrett and Chisum why he was making the trip to Lordsburg. 'If I don't get the jewellery back there ain't no real reason for me to go on to Lordsburg,' he finished lamely. And Pat Garrett silently chastised himself for doubting Mr

Trouble on the Lordsburg Trail 41

Howard's integrity.

'We'll try and sort out your problem in Tularosa, Mr Howard,' Mr Chisum said. 'Logan obviously knows I'm in the territory; it could only be him who set those men on to us, so there's no sense in me hiding my presence here any longer.' The rancher's face hardened. 'The only way Logan could have known I was making the trip to Tularosa would be through Stoker. Either he's changed his mind about wanting to talk to me and told Logan of our intended meeting. Logan would then reckon that he'd a golden opportunity to get rid of his only big rival in the cattle business in New Mexico.' Chisum bleak-smiled Garrett. 'Killing you, Pat, would seem like an extra bonus to the sonuvabitch. But what I fear is that Stoker spoke out of turn and thereby signed his own death warrant by Logan hearing of it. I think Stoker could be dead, as undoubtedly we would have been, Mr Howard, if it hadn't been for your quick thinking and fast gunplay. I'm beholden to you, Mr Howard.'

'I was saving my own neck as well, Mr Chisum,' Ben said, modest-voiced, but pleased that the killing of the men hadn't upset his guts, made him throw up in front of Garrett and Chisum. Not that he was getting a taste for killing. He had, he thought, just removed two sources of evil from God's sweet earth, and carried on thumbing out the smouldering pieces of cloth round the bullet hole in his coat.

'If Stoker is dead as you reckon, Mr Chisum,'

Garrett said, stern-faced. 'Then you can ride back to Lincoln with my deputies as escorts. Logan will send men to try and kill you again when he finds out he's failed this time. Getting shot at is my job, not yours. I'll hang around here, see if I can scout out the place where the illegal cattle trading is taking place between our friend Bill Bonney and whoever Logan's man is. Logan himself won't be up front doing the dealing, that's for sure. If I get a lead, or get real lucky by finding someone who is willing to talk to you about the rustling I'll send you a wire, Mr Chisum.'

'I said that I feared Stoker was dead, Pat,' Chisum said, beady-eyeing Garrett. 'Till I know for certain, your men when they ride back from Tularosa should prove if my fears are right or not. Till then I stay.'

Garrett, knowing Chisum's stubborn moods, didn't press his suggestion any further. Turning to Ben he said, 'I can only second Mr Chisum's thanks, Mr Howard. Your pa would have been real proud of you; he couldn't have bettered your style. But I'd ride on to Lordsburg if I was you. Shorty, won't be too happy at you gunning down his buddies and if he sees you around Tularosa he could sneak up on you and try even up the score.'

'I can't do that, Mr Garrett,' Ben said, stubborn-jawed. 'I can't go to my aunt's place without the jewellery. And I ain't going till I get Betsy back. I'll find some sort of a job in Tularosa to tide me over till I get back what's rightly mine.'

Garrett subjected Ben to a lengthy, studied

look. 'I could swear you in as a temporary deputy while I'm scouting the territory, Mr Howard. The pay isn't much though.' Garrett nodded to the dead gunmen. 'And as these *hombres* have just showed it's a job that attracts a heap of hostility to the holder of the badge. Don't get me wrong, Mr Howard, I'm not offering you the job as a goodwill handout for pulling me and Mr Chisum out of the shit. I need a good man to ride with me, to watch my back, because it seems that I'm a marked man in this part of the territory, and you're good. You've got your pa's lawman's blood running through you. You just think about taking the badge for a spell, give me your answer when you've made up your mind. Now I reckon we should start getting the dear departed buried then we can look around for their horses or you'll have to ride double with me, Mr Howard.' Garrett grinned. 'And that sure won't please my horse one little bit.'

FOUR

Shorty dismounted on the outskirts of Tularosa. It would be asking for trouble for him to be seen riding into town on a horse that men knew wasn't his own. Riding along his back-trail were the biggest cattleman in the south-west, a marshal who had killed everything from a buffalo to a man, and an unknown kid with a draw like greased-lightning. And they were all out for his blood. He would have to make himself scarce till they reckoned his trail had got too cold for them to follow. Keeping the horse would be a dead giveaway.

If the horse was too dangerous to keep the gear on its back wasn't. He unstrapped the saddle and slung it and the saddle-bags over his shoulder. Guessing that the old horse was the kid's, Chisum and Garrett wouldn't be seen dead up on such a flea-bitten animal, he stepped back and drew out his pistol and out of natural-born meanness and wanting to get back at the kid for killing Pena and Leroy, he fired two shells into the head of the grey, then walked the rest of the way into Tularosa.

Trouble on the Lordsburg Trail   45

* * *

Shorty, knocking urgently and noisily on the door of one of the upstairs private rooms in the Tularosa cathouse, brought a ballicky-naked Kerney to the door. Kerney favoured Shorty with a snake-eyed look for interrupting his pleasure. Shorty cast an envious glance past Kerney and glimpsed his boss's pleasure, equally unclothed, lying on the bed, the sheet hardly covering her at all. Knowing how near he had been ending dead alongside Pena and Leroy he matched Kerney's drop-dead scowl with one of his own and before Kerney could ask why the hell he had knocked him up he blurted out how things had gone dead wrong for them at Chisum's camp. Permanently so for Pena and Leroy.

'This sure-fire kid,' a pinched-assed-faced Kerney said, 'is he one of Billy the Kid's bunch of riders bought over by Chisum?'

'I don't know,' Shorty replied. 'I ain't seen him with the Kid when he brings the cattle down from Lincoln, but whoever he is he's real fast and sneaky with a pistol. The boys hadn't a chance and they were coverin' the sonuvabitch. He wasn't wearing a gunbelt, shirt carrying a pistol I reckon, that's what fooled them, and got themselves killed.'

'What have you done with the horse you said you borrowed?' Kerney asked. 'I don't want Garrett to trace you by finding it in the livery barn, remember the bastard knows what you look like.'

Shorty grinned. 'I shot the old walking bag of

bones outside of town and hoofed it in on foot.' He didn't mention to Kerney that the saddle and the rest of the gear was downstairs and the pieces of jewellery he had surprisingly found in the saddle-bags were in his pocket. He reckoned he had earned a little bonus for all the sweat he had lost by his brush with death.

'Good,' said Kerney. 'Now you get out to that abandoned line cabin on the south edge of Logan's spread. Lie low there till Garrett loses heart in looking for you and heads back to Lincoln. Use my horse. I'll get one of the boys to bring some supplies out to you.'

'OK,' said Shorty and grabbed one more tantalizing look at Kerney's girl before the door was slammed in his face. He made another call before leaving the building. At a door further along the hall.

'Jeeze,' the big-breasted blonde exclaimed who answered his knock. 'You know I don't start work this early, unless the fella's paid for an all-nighter.'

'I ain't payin' you a social call, honey,' Shorty said, wishing that he could stay as he mentally licked his lips at the blood-rousing sight of so much soft, bare flesh. But he knew he couldn't perform at his best no matter how much the blonde encouraged him. Pena and Leroy's manner of dying and the threat coming along behind him was concentrating Shorty's mind on more serious matters, such as preventing himself from suffering the same fate. 'I'm ridin' out of town for a few days,' he said. 'I kinda thought that you'd like to wear these the next time I call.' He handed the blonde the jewellery.

The girl blinked the sleep out of her eyes and examined the rings and necklace. She knew enough about jewellery to know that the pieces, though pretty, weren't very valuable. A penny-ante asshole of a thief like Shorty wouldn't come by real pricy jewellery. Still, she thought, they would go well with her green dress.

'Gee, thanks, Shorty,' she said. She bent down and gave him a cold-lipped kiss on his cheek. 'Now you push off and let me get back to sleep, I'm dead on my feet. The Bar X boys were in the place last night and worked the butts of us girls. I'll see you when you get back into town.' Then she shut the door in Shorty's face.

A sour-gutted Shorty walked downstairs thinking of the pleasant time Kerney was having while he was heading out to a draughty, flea-ridden cabin in the middle of nowhere. But Kerney had lost all interest in the pleasuring game, he was doing some serious thinking.

'Ain't you comin' under the sheet, Kerney?' the redhead said plaintively. 'It's gettin' kinda chilly in here.'

'Shut up!' Kerney snarled. 'I'm thinkin'!'

He was thinking that to be able to hang on to the money Logan had laid out he would have to try a second attempt to kill Chisum and Garrett. A dangerous undertaking; the bastards would be on their guard now. Yet it went against all his business ethics to give money back once he had got his hands around it. To keep the money and do nothing was more dangerous. Logan couldn't exactly shout it about that the man he had paid good money to kill Chisum had welshed on the deal but some of Logan's hard-assed crew would pay him a midnight visit and he would end up like Stoker, lying dead in a dark alley.

This time the proposed killing of Chisum and Garrett would have to be more carefully planned, Kerney thought, as he pulled on his pants. Not only would he have Garrett and Chisum alerted to meet any trouble, the deadly-shooting kid had to be considered, real hard, or a few more of his boys would end up biting the dust. He finally decided that he would only send one man out, to spy on the Chisum party. Find out if the three deputies Shorty had seen ride out of the camp had returned. Where they were worried him. Garrett wouldn't have come this far south with only a kid, even a fast-draw one, to watch over Chisum. His deputies would be nosing around someplace.

He knew what Chisum's next move would be, to call on Stoker. Kerney's lips curled back in a slight but smug smile. Chisum would find out that he had busted his balls riding all the way here from Lincoln for sweet damn all. His knifing of Stoker had put paid to that lead to Logan.

Once fully dressed he buckled on his gunbelt then leaning over the bed slapped the redhead's bare ass in a playful parting gesture and left her room to issue orders that should keep him in the money and Chisum and Garrett well and truly dead.

FIVE

Kirsty watched the Tularosa deputy sheriff ride back along the trail to town. He had brought her the news that her stepfather had been found knifed to death in an alley. His body had been taken to the funeral parlour and that the sheriff would be obliged if she would come into town to formally identify it. Then the mortician could go ahead with the funeral arrangements she wanted for her stepfather. The deputy also told her that no one had been arrested for the killing and that there were no clues to who it could have been.

She had thanked the deputy and told him that she would come into town as soon as she had fed and watered the stock. Kirsty would naturally have been shocked and upset on hearing of the murder, or sudden death by accident, of anyone she closely knew, but not in this case. She thought that going to an early grave couldn't have happened to a more suitable candidate. Kirsty was only surprised someone hadn't put Stoker there sooner. She had threatened to do so. She hated and loathed her stepfather. He had been an idle drunken bully. She couldn't understand what her mother had seen in him to take him as her husband, share her bed with him not six months after her real pa had died of the wasting sickness.

Stoker had let the farm go, growing fields unattended, barns dropping to pieces for the lack of repairs, and relying on her and her kid brother to tend to the farm animals. What money he had coming in was from sort of cattle-dealing, which, she had thought, knowing her stepfather's shifty character, was dishonest, the money not spent on the farm but in the saloons and whorehouses in Tularosa.

The young men who had driven the cattle down from the north were real fine boys. Raised their hats to her, bowing at the waist, 'Yes ma'amed' her when she offered to make them coffee. The other men who occasionally visited Stoker, older men, were vicious, cruel-eyed visaged men. What business Stoker had with them she didn't rightly know, but they frightened her, especially the one called Pena. His eyes used to strip her naked, making her flesh creep.

Her stepfather had the same blood-chilling wants when liquored up. He would seemingly accidently rub against her ass when brushing past her as she worked in the kitchen. Or try to squeeze her breasts when serving him a meal when her ma wasn't in the room. One night he sneaked into her room when she had been fast asleep. Her ma was out of the house, sitting up with a sick neighbour. Kirsty shuddered, still smelling the whiskey-laden breath and the rank body sweat, then she smiled slightly. She had sounded and acted a lot braver than she really was.

She always slept with her pa's old Remington .44 pistol under her pillow. He had given it to her when she had only been eleven or so, nigh on eight years ago. It had taken all her strength, using both thumbs to cock the heavy pistol. It had been her defence in the likelihood of an Indian attack on the farm. Indian trouble was rife in the territory those days and young white girls a much sought after prize by the raiding bucks. Fortunately she had never had to use the pistol, till that night, and not against a red man but a so-called white.

The weight of Stoker's body pressing on her had woken her up. In an instant she had reached for the pistol and thrust the muzzle hard into his left ear so that he could hear the click of the hammer being drawn back real loud. And in language unfitting for a church meeting hall choirgirl she had said, 'You dirty sonuvabitch, if you don't get out of my room, *pronto*, I'll blow your sick brains clear through your skull. And if you don't stop hitting my ma I'll pistol-whip you, so help me God.' He had got off her bed and out of her room as though his pants had caught fire. Her threat had worked. He had never pestered her or struck her ma since that night.

She could have left the farm, thought long and hard about doing so. She could have got a job waiting-on in one of the eating-houses in

Tularosa, but once the threat of the Remington had gone Stoker would have gone back to his old mean ways and started beating up her ma again. When her ma had died she had still been tied to the farm. She had a kid brother, Jonathan, named after his pa, only eight years old. She couldn't earn enough money, to keep them both. There was even a stronger reason for her not leaving the farm, by blood-line the place belonged to her and Jonathan, in no way was Stoker going to get his dirty hands on the deeds. One day Stoker might fall off his horse when drunk and break his neck. Till that hopeful event happened there had been an uneasy sort of a truce between them, backed up by the Remington, carried now slung about her waist in her pa's gunbelt whenever Stoker was on the farm.

Kirsty gazed on what was hers now by birthright. It wasn't much. Too run down for her and an eight-year-old boy to bring up to shape so that they could get a living from it. The only thing she could do was to try and sell the place, use the money for her and Jonathan to go back East to her pa's folks. Kirsty closed her lips in two thin, determined lines. One thing was for sure, Stoker wasn't coming back to the farm to be buried beside her ma and pa in the family burial plot. He could find a resting place among the other drunks and bullies on Boot Hill.

'Jonathan!' she yelled. 'Get the mule hitched up to the buggy. I've got to go into town!' She picked up the two pails of feed and water and stepped off the porch. Feeding live hogs came long before tending to a dead pig.

Pat Garrett, riding point, saw the dust of riders coming along the trail from the direction of Tularosa. 'Men coming!' he called over his shoulder. 'Could be more trouble headin' our way. if it is we'll meet it head on.' Drawing his mount to a halt he pulled out his Winchester and dismounted, Ben and Mr Chisum doing likewise. The three of them spread themselves across the trail, rifles held high across their chests, fingers taking up the first pressure on the triggers, Ben figuring that he would be as old and grey-haired with worry as Mr Chisum before he made it to Lordsburg. Unless, he thought morbidly, he was destined to die young. On hearing Pat Garrett's, 'It's OK, it's my deputies,' his screwed-up stomach unwound somewhat, opining, a little more hopefully, that his time hadn't arrived yet.

John Chisum listened grim-faced to the news the deputies had brought back from Tularosa. It was as he had feared, Stoker was dead.

'He was knifed in some alley, Mr Chisum,' Bert, the senior of the deputies said. 'The sheriff is putting it about that he came off the worst in a drunken brawl. Though witnesses say he'd been hittin' the bottle hard on his ownsome. But he was makin' his mouth go about you, Mr Chisum, payin' him a visit. So I reckon, in spite what the local law say you can give a calculatin' guess who paid the man who stuck the knife in Stoker.'

Trouble on the Lordsburg Trail

Chisum heaped silent but profane curses on Logan's head. He had himself killed men, in defence of his life, while he was building up his herd, but he always faced the men with a gun. Ordering the dark-alley stabbing of a drunk was dirty tactics. Cold-blooded murder no less. 'Has Mr Stoker left any kin?' he asked.

'A girl and a young boy I heard,' replied Bert. He pointed back along the trail. 'There's a cutoff track back a piece, Mr Chisum, that leads to the Stoker holding. You can't miss it. There's a dead horse there, what's left of it, a big grey by the look of what the buzzards and crows haven't eaten. It musta broke its leg and its owner put a slug in it to put it out of its misery cause there ain't no sign of any saddle and gear lyin' around.'

Garrett glanced at Ben to see how he was taking the news of the killing of his horse. He had never seen a boy grow up into a man so quickly before. At the camp he had been a youth, a fast-gun kid. Now his face was hardening, merciless, Indian-looking. Shorty was a dead man if Mr Howard ever caught up with him, he thought.

'I'll take that badge, Mr Garrett,' Ben said, voice as unyielding as his face. 'When I face the sonuvabitch who killed Betsy I want to shoot him within the law as my pa would have done.'

The kid had really grown up into a *bueno hombre*, Garrett opined with satisfaction. His great loss hadn't turned him into a bitter-souled manhunter. There was hope for law and order coming to New Mexico in spite of all the shooting going on around Lincoln.

'Some riders comin' in, Sis,' Jonathan shouted from the front porch. Kirsty hurriedly loosened the strap on the mule and led it out of the buggy's shafts, letting it walk over to the water trough on its own as she ran to the house, bundling her brother inside with her. The identifying of her stepfather's body and the burial arrangements had not taken long and in no time at all the buggy was raising the dust back along the trail to the farm, Stoker forgotten as though he had never set foot on the place.

When Kirsty stepped out on to the porch again she cradled a double-barrelled shotgun in her arms and the Remington sagged low in its sheath at her right hip. She had told Jonathan to stay indoors and keep away from the windows, waiting with apprehension till she could make out who the riders were. It was a dangerous stance she was taking and she didn't want her brother to come to any harm because of her foolhardiness. But she meant to start as she intended running the farm. If the riders were the Mexican and some of his men she would tell them that she didn't want to see their dirty hides on her land again. What dealings they'd had with Stoker were buried with him on Boot Hill.

How could she hope to sell the place, Kirsty reasoned, if cattle-rustlers used it as a place of business? She didn't think too long or too deeply

Trouble on the Lordsburg Trail 57

that they were men who couldn't be scared off by a young girl armed with a shotgun that was liable to burst its barrels if fired and an old cannon of a pistol. But Kirsty told herself that she was the man about the place now and she had to make a stand like one. The riders drew up several feet from the porch and as the dust of their coming settled she counted six of them. Men she had not seen before. One, a burly man, wearing a white linen duster seemed to Kirsty to have the look of the bossman. Next to him was a tall gangly-legged man. The third rider, a po-faced boy not much older than she was. The back three riders were noncommittal-faced men. Whoever they were they didn't have the look of men who scared easily.

The starting was harder than she had thought but putting on a bold face, and with fire in her voice, Kirsty said, 'My stepfather's dead; I'm running the farm now so there'll be no more cattle trading done on my land. Even if you say you have genuine bills of sale for the cattle. So quit my land right now!' She swung the shotgun round and covered the riders with it, controlling her blind panic by mumbling a silent prayer.

Ben shrunk down in his saddle. Looking at things realistically he supposed he could have foreseen trouble from gun-toting assholes like Pena riding across one of the wildest and lawless stretches of territory in the Union. The likely possibility of getting peppered from a shotgun held by a loco-eyed girl wasn't a trail hazard he could have even dreamed about meeting up with.

A second look at her got Ben thinking that she didn't look like a girl. Hair cut short, as though the mule drinking at the trough had chewed at it, and a figure that showed none of the bumps and curves a fella expected a girl to have. Of course, he charitably conceded, the gear she wore, baggy, well-patched pants, and a shirt that would look big on a man twice her build, wasn't the best of clothes to show a girl to her best advantage.

Garrett wasn't interested in the girl's figure, or lack of one, he was more concerned about the shotgun in the hands of an obviously unstable female. In an attempt to put her at ease before her nervous fingers yanked at the triggers he said, 'We're lawmen from Lincoln, miss. I'm Sheriff Garrett, this is Mr Chisum, he owns the Jingle Bob ranch; you've m'be heard of him. The rest are my deputies so there isn't any need to be holding that scattergun on us.' He finished by favouring Kirsty with a big friendly smile.

Chisum raised his hat to Kirsty. 'We have ridden to Tularosa to put a stop to those cattle deals you mention. It's been my cattle, stolen I might add, they've been dealing in. Your late stepfather was prepared to name the man at the back of the transactions. It's on my account he got killed so please accept my condolences. I'll see to it that you won't lose out having the breadwinner taken away from you.' Chisum matched Garrett's smile. 'Now if you'd allow me and my men to step down and water our horses and brew some coffee while we talk things over I'd be most obliged.'

Kirsty's face gradually lost its wild look. 'My stepfather isn't any loss, Mr Chisum. And he brought damn all money in. So don't have any regrets, on both accounts, for me.' Kirsty lowered the shotgun. 'You're welcome to step down and see to your horses and there's no need for you to fuss around lighting a fire for your coffee, there's a stove inside you can use.'

'Thank you, miss. That's most Christian-like of you,' Garrett said, more than somewhat relieved as he swung down from the saddle.

Ben took a farm-bred youth's look around him as he dismounted. Whatever else the dead Stoker had professed to be, he thought, farming wasn't one of his long suits. The whole place was falling to bits. His gaze took in the girl again. She looked in keeping with the general state of her farm. A good scrub down in a hot tub and some more feminine-looking clothes wouldn't come amiss.

Kirsty saw the lip-curling look of disdain the younger of the deputies was giving her. She blushed angrily. M'be she had let her appearance slip a little of late, and still covered in the dust of her ride to Tularosa didn't make her look any prettier. But that didn't give the smug-faced lawman the right to look down his nose at her. How did he know what it was like to run a farm and look after a kid brother? And keep a drunken horn dog at arm's length? Curl that lip at me again, she thought resolutely, and lawman or not you'll get a single load of buckshot in your pants. Even if you are right about the way I look.

Kirsty suddenly found her femininity again. The natural urge to dress like the girl she was. To fix her hair so that it didn't look such a fright. And m'be on special occasions, a dab of her ma's sweet-smelling perfume between her breasts and the backs of her ears. But it was too far ahead thinking, hoping of such pleasant happenings right now. And to have dressed up and used perfume when her stepfather had been around would have set him thinking that she had done it to excite him, inviting him to have his way with her.

Telling Jonathan to see to their unexpected callers when they came inside she almost ran into the kitchen. She lifted the big pan of water, hardly warm, off the stove and staggering under its weight made her way to what her pa had called the bathroom, a tongue and grooved, planked and tarp hut attached to one end of the house. She hadn't the time to fill the iron tub for a real soaking so she had to make do with the water just reaching her ankles. Not a bath at all but an all-over wash. Shivering in the tepid water she began to soap herself.

The deputies were sitting on the front porch sipping at their coffees, drawing on their pipes or makings. Garrett was telling Mr Chisum that if he rode back to Lincoln, as he had advised him to do, he and Mr Howard would work out from the farm. If the girl would be willing to let them use it as a base. It seemed wiser and healthier, Garrett said, to keep well away from Tularosa for the time being. The lawman took Chisum's single grunt as his acceptance of his plan and would ride north.

Ben was leaning on the corral fencing, aimlessly eyeing the four horses in the compound, still feeling low in spirits over the loss of Betsy. Jonathan tugging at his jacket brought his thoughts back from thinking of the great satisfaction he would get throwing down on the man who had killed Betsy, to the present.

'My sis, Kirsty, has a pistol like that, Mr Howard,' Jonathan said, touching the butt of the Navy. 'Have you shot any outlaws with it?'

Ben smiled down at him. While they had been in the kitchen making the coffee the boy had asked them all their names and had told them his, but it was the first time he had heard the girl's name. Kirsty; a fine and sweet-sounding name, he thought. Though the girl looked anything but sweet and fine. Then Ben began to wonder where she had got to. There had been no sign of her since she had spoken to them on the porch. Was she unsociable as well as highly strung?

'Have you, being a deputy, shot dead any outlaws?' repeated Jonathan.

'I ain't really a proper deputy,' Ben replied. 'I'm just a farm boy like you. Though I've had to shoot several men who were intent on killing me.' Ben's face stoned over. 'And there's another fella I've got lined up for killing if I ever catch up with him.'

'My sis nearly killed my step-pa with her pistol,' Jonathan said proudly. 'I heard her tell him so this night he snucked into her room. He used to hit my ma, and me sometimes, but he never did after that night. Kirsty must have thrown a scare into him. And Sis tole me I'm not called Jonathan Stoker any more. I'm Jonathan Pringle after my real pa again.'

Ben looked at the boy with wide-eyed disbelief but by the seriousness of Jonathan's expression he hadn't been relating a pack of lies or childlike make-believe happenings. Stoker, he concluded, must have been one helluva son-of-a-bitch, beating up his wife and trying to get his way with his stepdaughter. He was now lying in a place he well deserved. Then Ben cursed himself for his wrongly held first impressions of the girl. She'd had more pressing and worrying things on her mind than dressing up pretty.

'Your stepfather wasn't a nice man to have around, Jonathan,' he said. 'Now you're the man about the place you'll have to work real hard to help your sister make a go of the farm. That fella who called himself your pa certainly didn't pull his weight. I had a farm, way up north of here, in the Nations, but I hadn't a sister to help me to run the place so I had to sell up.'

Jonathan's telling him of his ma's beating and the near rape of his sister settled Ben's own troubles somewhat. Put the loss of Betsy and the jewellery in perspective. A minor upset in his life compared to what Stoker had put his adopted family through. Though that didn't mean he wasn't going to draw on the man who had shot Betsy if he ever crossed trails with him again. He put an arm round Jonathan's shoulders. 'Come on, sodbuster,' he said. 'Let's go an' see if those hard-riding *hombres* sitting on your front porch have left some coffee in the pot.'

SIX

A still damp-skinned Kirsty got dressed as hastily as her bath had been. She didn't want to go to all the trouble of dressing up only to find that the man she was really doing it for had ridden off. That, Kirsty Pringle, she thought bitterly, would serve you right for letting your pride get the better of you.

She took a final, quick, critical look at herself in the mirror. Her sun-bronzed, freckled face was something she could do nothing about to improve its appearance, nor her cropped-short brown hair with corn-yellow streaks running through it, bleached by the same sun. To make her look prettier she would have to have weeks of treatment of the fancy creams and lotions she had seen in the mail order catalogues. Her blue, white collar-edged dress, was her favourite, but now showing more of her legs than was decent since the last time she had worn it. Kirsty's eyes moistened. She had been the belle of the homesteaders' dance that year, boys crowding round her for a dance. Now, she opined, she looked like one of the painted ladies who entertained the men in the saloons in Tularosa. Damnit, she thought angrily, the mournful-faced boy would laugh this time when she showed herself on the porch. Kirsty rubbed her eyes dry with the back of her hand and mentally gritting her teeth, walked as casually as her strung-up nerves allowed her to, out on to the porch.

There was a hurried scrambling on to feet and the raising of hats by the men on the porch as Kirsty came up to them. Ben stopped in his stride and gawped like a dumb-struck backwoods hillbilly, hardly believing he was looking at the same girl who had held the shotgun on them. She had all the right curves and bumps, and then some, any man could wish to see. Following the rest of the herd he took off his hat and feasted his eyes on the transformed Kirsty, his morose feelings over the loss of Betsy rapidly receding.

'I hope Jonathan has been seeing to you and your men's needs, Mr Chisum,' Kirsty said, sweet-smiling at the rancher.

'Just fine, miss, just fine,' Chisum replied, wishing that he had been forty years younger. Sparking up to the girl would have been a whole heap more pleasant than night-nursing a bunch of longhorns as he was doing those days as he built up his spread. 'I'd be most obliged if we could impose on your generosity still further, Miss....'

'Kirsty Pringle, Mr Chisum,' Kirsty said. 'I've taken my pa's name again.'

'Miss Kirsty,' Chisum began again. 'As I told you, me and my men came here to put an end to the underhand cattle dealing between a certain party in Tularosa and Mr William Bonney; you may have heard of him by his other name, Billy the Kid. With your step ... with Stoker being silenced I've no proof to convince a court of law, or even a cattleman's court, that this party in Tularosa is buying cattle he knows is stolen. Mr Garrett and his deputy, young Mr Howard there, are staying in the territory to see if they can come up with any leads on the men who bring the cattle here, where they eventually end up, whose grass they're grazing on. Me and the rest of the deputies are riding back to Lincoln. What Mr Garrett would like is your permission to use your farm as his base.'

'We'll feed ourselves, Miss Kirsty,' Garrett said. 'Sleep in one of your barns, so we won't be a burden to you. And naturally we'll pay for the use of it and, of course, for any feed and grain our horses need.' He could have added that, Mr Howard, in his spare time, would repair your broken-down fencing. The eyeballing the kid was giving her, Garrett reckoned, he would be willing to rebuild the whole farm, house, barns, hogpen, whatever, all for free if she kept up with her sweet-smiling. 'If it's not to your liking us staying, Miss Kirsty,' he continued, 'just say so, no offence will be taken and we'll ride on to Tularosa.'

'Why it's no trouble to me at all having you and Mr Howard stay, Mr Garrett,' Kirsty said. 'But I insist that I do the cooking when you're on the farm.' Kirsty turned and looked directly at Ben.

'And I'll mend that burn hole in your coat, Mr Howard.' Face all sweet and innocent-like she added, 'Did you stumble into your campfire in the dark?'

Garrett, Chisum and the deputies grinned widely; Ben stopped his gawking and coloured up, realizing that the girl was ribbing him, getting some of her own back sensing the way he had looked down his nose at her at the way she had been dressed the first time he had seen her. John Chisum came to the rescue of his hurt pride.

'Mr Howard saved my and Mr Garrett's lives this morning,' he said. 'Shot dead two desperadoes. Had to fire at 'em through his coat. That's how the hole came about, Miss Kirsty. I promised to buy the boy a new one in Tularosa.'

Kirsty felt suddenly deflated. All she could come out with was a weak, apologetic, 'Oh!' but thinking that for the second time Mr Howard had made her look small. What was annoying her most was that she had just said that she would cook his meals for him. She did however feel some satisfaction in the way he was ogling her. So getting dressed up hadn't been a waste of her time. Though that was no great conquest. Small, shabbily-dressed, Mr Howard wouldn't sweep a girl off her feet with his looks that was for sure. He wouldn't warrant any girl giving him a second look. It was puzzling her why she had gone to the bother of smartening herself up for him.

On hearing of his shooting dead two outlaws, Kirsty did just that, gave Ben a second, much longer look. She noticed a determination and directness in his features she had missed before. It affected her in a way she couldn't understand, causing her to lower her gaze. Damnit, she thought, he's getting me all confused again. Kirsty mumbled some excuse about having to see to some chore or other and asking Jonathan to give her a hand, hurried back inside the house.

Ben was having confused feelings as well. How could a girl he had only just met get his goat so easily? He wasn't staying long enough in the territory to have any interest in her at all, other than the normal interest a boy would have on seeing a pretty girl.

Garrett was weighing up the looks that were passing between them and, experienced in such matters, he opined even if they didn't know it at this point in time, they were building up a relationship with each other. That worried him. He and the kid were about to ride out on a dangerous trail and they would have to be alert and quick reacting as a hostile buck to danger or they would end up dead. Although the kid had proved himself cool and deadly under pressure he still wasn't a full-blooded manhunter. That skill only came by experience. And the kid would never live long enough to gain that know-how if his mind was clouded with thoughts of the girl. If he had to die, reasoned Garrett, he didn't want it to be because the man who was supposed to be watching his back was mooning, or whatever, over a slip of a girl he had just met. The sooner they left the farm and got scouting the more settled he would be.

'I think it best that you start heading back to Lincoln now, Mr Chisum,' he said. 'Logan has the edge over us; the sooner me and Mr Howard try and take the war to him the quicker we can resolve what we came to Tularosa for.'

'I know you're right, Pat,' Chisum replied, doubtful voiced. 'That's why I've decided to go back; it'll give you and Mr Howard a freer hand as you won't have my hide to worry about. But I still feel that I'm running out on you, letting you both fight my battles.'

'Meaning no disrespect, Mr Chisum,' Ben said. 'But I'm not fighting your battles. I'm wearing this badge for strictly personal reasons.'

Garrett grinned. 'And no disrespect from me, Mr Chisum, because I'm not fighting your battles either. I'm only doing my duty as a lawman hunting down killers and cattle-thieves.'

Chisum smiled. 'You two sons-of-bitches have got me hog-tied.' His smile went and the hard, unyielding face of Chisum the riding-tall man showed through. 'But if you need any help, you just holler, Pat. I'll come fireballing down here, Texas style,' he growled. 'With half my herd and stomp that dirty-dealing sonuvabitch Logan into the ground. One thing more,' voice and face lightening, 'see that Deputy Howard gets that new coat I owe him.'

SEVEN

'They've got themselves a real sweet operation going here, Mr Howard,' Pat Garrett said. 'Billy and his boys bring the cattle down through that rough country away to our right, well clear of any regular cattle trails. Drive them into this wash somewhere ahead of us and push them along till they're on Stoker's land, where we are now. All out of sight of any prying eyes. There is enough water and grass down there to feed twenty or thirty longhorns.'

'Why doesn't Billy the Kid just drive the cattle straight on to Logan's range, cut out the middleman, Stoker?'

'Because this spot is a nice out-of-the-way place for Logan's men to change the brand marks on the beef. It wouldn't be wise for him, an upright citizen of the State of New Mexico with his big ambitions, to be caught altering brands on his home range by a Cattlemen's Association inspector doing a snap check on his herd.' Garrett pointed down into the wash. 'There, you can see the remains of the branding-iron fires.'

Trouble on the Lordsburg Trail 71

* * *

They were, according to what Kirsty had told them, on the western edge of her land; land, because of the big wash that slashed right through it and the density of the brush, even her father had never bothered to plough over. She also told them that though she had never actually seen any of the cattle she had met the young men, who, she opined, had driven the cattle to the farm. Pleasant, good-mannered men she said, bold-eyeing Ben significantly. That was no news to Garrett. Everyone in Lincoln County knew that Billy the Kid and his polite band of young *pistoleros* were helping themselves to the Jingle Bob cattle. Kirsty then said that there were other men who called at the farm to see Stoker, led by a Mexican called Pena. She didn't know if they had anything to do with the stolen cattle but they were definitely not honest ranch-hands. And they had really scared her.

'That sonuva.... that fella Pena won't scare you again, Miss Kirsty,' Garrett said. 'Right now he's doing his scaring in hell. Sent there by Mr Howard.' Garrett grinned at her. 'Ruined his coat doing it.'

Ben did some cocky smirking of his own, and again Kirsty knew that she had come off second best. She began to wonder why it was she was allowing a boy, just passing through, to get under her skin.

* * *

'We can't do anything out here at present, Mr Howard,' Garrett said. 'Though we'll keep a watch on the place. I'm betting that Billy don't know that Stoker is dead and will still be driving his ill-gotten gains to the usual rendezvous. I'm also banking on Logan sending someone out to tell Billy about the new arrangements for branding the cattle. He'll not take the risk that the new owner of the farm will turn a blind eye to having rustled cows on her property, he's got too much at stake. Our move will be to be here when Billy shows up and see who comes to meet him and plan it from there. We'll have time; the cattle will be bedded down here for a few days.' Garrett pulled his horse round from the wash. 'In the meantime let's head for Tularosa and buy you that new coat. M'be, if we're lucky, we'll bump into Shorty.' Garrett grinned. 'But before you plug him give me time to question him. If Mr Chisum's right about Logan's murderous intentions towards him the sonuvabitch could tell me if there are any more like him who do Logan's dirty work.'

They had hardly cleared the wash when six riders suddenly came bursting out of the thick brush and surrounded them. Ben's hand snaked for his pistol now sheathed in Pena's gunbelt he had fastened about his middle. With his inborn ability to handle guns Ben found that after a few practice draws he could aim, shoot as fast as he could when his pistol was stuck in the top of his pants, and feel a great deal more comfortable. Garrett, stone-faced laid a restrainig hand on his arm.

'Howdy Billy, Charlie, Dave,' Garrett said. 'I'm not familiar with the names of the rest of you boys but I reckon I'll find them printed on some Wanted flyer.'

Billy, leaning easily on his saddle-horn, favoured Garrett with a twisted bucktoothed grin. 'Hirin' school-kids as deputies now, Pat?' he said mockingly. 'He don't look strong enough to heave that big cannon out of its sheath let alone aim and fire it.'

Garrett held his peace. Billy was a man of unpredictable moods. He could shoot the pair of them out of hand, or equally let them go. He just smiled at Billy and took the ribbing as though he was enjoying it. Ben was more forthcoming. He had lost enough since coming to New Mexico and he wasn't about to have his pride taken away as well by being made to look small by a bunch of ragged-assed cow-thieves no older than him. That riled him. Kirsty's attempted down-putting of him was different: she was a girl and knew no better. He gave Billy a frozen-eyed look.

'I'm on my way to Lordsburg to visit my kinfolk, a farm boy hailin' from the Nations,' he said, voice as steeled over as his face. 'Watching my manners, causing no trouble to anyone at all. Even avoided towns so as to keep clear of any possible trouble. Since crossing the Pegos, however, four men took it in their minds, for one reason or another, to cause me grief. I killed three of them, pistol-whipped the other. Now you're trying to stomp on me. If it's in your mind to push it to a shoot-out, Mr Bonney, just do it and we'll get it done with, one way or the other.'

Billy laughed out aloud. Screwing ass in his saddle he eyed his broad-grinning companions. 'Boys,' he said, 'we've netted ourselves a genuine town-taming *hombre*.' Facing Ben again, still all smiles, he said. 'Are you fast enough to take the six of us on, mister?'

'Now it would be downright foolish of me to think I could to that, Mr Bonney,' Ben said. 'But I tell you this, I'll kill you and that shifty-eyed fella alongside you before I go down. And I'll do it even if I'm dead, and that's a fact, Mr Bonney. So if you don't want a real battle on your hands you and your boys just back off and let me and Mr Garrett go on our way.'

Billy's smile sickened as his eyes narrowed with the intensity of the gaze he was focusing on his challenger, as if trying to read his mind, whether Garrett's deputy was trying a high-risk bluff or in deadly earnest. Billy, a master in the high-risk bluff stakes himself, came to the quick conclusion that it was no bluff. It was as the deputy had stated, a fact. Ben waited, watching for so much as a twitching finger on Billy's gun hand, cool and clear-headed, which surprised him. It was as though his pa was standing at his side backing his play. If Billy's hand moved he was a dead man he told himself with growing confidence of his fast-draw capabilities.

Garrett could hear a lot of squeaking leather as asses shuffled nervously in their saddles. Instead of just standing sweating he decided to raise the ante still higher. Prove to Billy, if the harebrained kid hadn't already grasped it, that he had lost his edge. Young Mr Howard had snatched it away from him. He was his pa's son all right. 'To put the situation more clearly to you, Billy,' he said, 'as old as I am I reckon I can take two more of you with me to wherever I'm bound for in the life hereafter. So it looks like if it comes to a shooting there'll not be enough of us standing to see the dead decently buried. Why don't we make it a Mexican standoff, Billy? There's no business for you here now to fight for. Stoker's dead and the new owner don't want shady cattle deals done on her land. Reckons she's calling the law in to put a stop to it. Take those cattle you've got bedded down somewhere near back to Mr Chisum where they belong. Then, when I finally put you behind bars, this is one less cattle-lifting charge that can be held against you.'

Charlie Bowdre, the rider Ben had called shifty-eyed put an end to Billy's savage, lower lip-chewing thinking. 'We ain't come all this way to start a war, Billy. There's one goin' on already in Lincoln. Let's get to hell out of it, find another buyer for the beef.'

'Charlie's talking sense, Billy,' Garrett said. 'Let's not spoil a nice day by a whole mess of killing.'

Billy gave his lip a rest and shot Ben a grim-faced scowl. 'You hold all the aces this time, *amigos*, but there'll be other hands, you can bet on it. OK boys, let's *vamoose!*' With horses kicking up the dust Billy and his boys disappeared into the brush as quickly as they had appeared.

Garrett let out his breath in one deep sighing gasp. 'Deputy Howard,' he said, 'you did the right thing pushing Billy to the brink, forcing him to rethink his position. But I'll have to admit that it scared the shit out of me.'

'It's as you said, Mr Garrett,' a straight-faced Ben said. 'You're an old man.'

'You're right,' replied Garrett. 'And if I don't put Billy where he can do no more harm soon I'm not much likely to get any older.' He grinned at Ben. 'But first things first, let's go and get you that new coat.'

EIGHT

Plummer, a squat, heavily whiskered, big-bellied man, thought once more of the dead Pena and Leroy. And of Shorty, still crapping himself in a line cabin at his lucky escape from sharing the same fate as his buddies. He drew up his horses and reaching into his saddle-bags pulled out a three-quarters full bottle of whiskey and putting it to his lips took three effortless gulps that almost emptied the bottle. He gasped as the raw liquor hit his stomach and brought tears to his eyes. Then he felt the fiery, well-being glow creep over him, relaxing his pinched-assed look somewhat.

Plummer's drinking wasn't a belated farewell salute to *compadres* sorely missed who had shared the dangers and risks of the owlhoot trail. He didn't give a shit about Pena and Leroy getting plugged. What was troubling his mind was that he could end up the same way, dead. His drinking was to stiffen up his spine and resolve, as an Indian buck would down firewater to work himself up before going out on a white-eyes killing raid.

If Pena, the meanest man with a gun he had ever known, could be caught short by the kid Shorty had told Kerney about, what chance had he if he came face to face with the kid? And Pena had held a gun on the kid, with Leroy backing him up. Pat Garrett on his own was a *pistolero* well out of his league, unless he could bushwhack him. Shorty had also told Kerney that the three deputies had left Chisum's camp but like Kerney he believed that they were still in the territory, close by. They would be West Texans, from the Panhandle. Hard men, unfeeling men. *Hombres* who would shoot a man laying flowers on his mother's grave if they held papers for him.

Kerney had told him that he had only to check on where Chisum and Garrett were, see if the deputies had shown up then ride back to town to tell him how things stood. If they looked favourable to them he would round up the rest of the boys and ride out to earn their fee. And that was the nearest he was going to get to Chisum and Garrett and the fast-shooting kid, Plummer earnestly thought, observe them from beyond Winchester range.

Plummer finished off the rest of the whiskey and threw the bottle away. Breaking wind at both ends he headed towards the Stoker farm. Kerney said that the farm would be the first place Chisum and Garrett would pay a call. They could still be there: if not Stoker's stepdaughter might know where the lawmen were. He had seen Stoker's stepdaughter in town getting supplies. She looked untouched. He would definitely enjoy making her talk if she proved a mite stubborn. Plummer ran his tongue over dry lips at the pleasant thought, experiencing a tightness in his throat and groin that were not liquor induced.

Kirsty had had a busy afternoon. She had rushed around doing only the essential chores on the farm before going to the big trunk in her bedroom and taking out three of her dresses. She let the hems down on them to a more respectable length as befitting a well-raised farm girl. Then, with Jonathan's help she had filled the tub for her to have a proper bath after which she sent him to feed the hens and make himself generally useful till she had her bath. Now she was stretched full out in the tub, soaking into her limbs its mind-relaxing heat. Thinking that all in all it had been a good day for her. Stoker's death had lifted a frightening burden from her shoulders. She and Jonathan could start shaping their new lives now. Her first step into her new future would be to keep wearing dresses again, except of course for the real dirty chores on the farm.

Even though she knew she would never be classed as beautiful, Kirsty felt a glow of feminine pride and satisfaction that Mr Chisum and his men must have found her at least attractive in some way by the fact that they had all got to their feet and raised their hats to her. Kirsty blushed then giggled, unless it was because she was showing her legs practically all the way up to her drawers. Mr Howard's eyes were nearly popping out of his head as though he had never seen a girl's bare legs before. Then she began to wonder why she should bother what he thought about her, and couldn't come up with an answer. Made her further think that Mr Howard, even though he wasn't here, could still somehow irritate her.

As she was standing out of the bath drying her hair, Kirsty suddenly heard the creaking of the porch boards caused by much heavier and longer-striding feet than Jonathan's. Startled, she froze for a moment in time, holding her breath, listening. Had Mr Howard returned to the farm, found out from Jonathan that she was having a bath and was now sneaking along the porch to have a peek at her while she had her clothes off? Then she immediately scolded herelf for thinking such unkind and wicked thoughts about Mr Howard.

Plummer, seeing no one about on the farm had dismounted and knocked on the front door. Getting no answer to his rapping he walked along the porch to see if anyone was working out back. Curious, he stopped outside the shack at the end of the porch and tried the latch and discovering that the door was unlocked, he pushed it open.

Kirsty heard the snick of the door latch being lifted and came to life again. She dropped the towel and grabbed the pistol from the chair next to the bath and holding it steady in both hands, pointed it at the door. She thumbed back the hammer and held her breath, the blood pounding

Trouble on the Lordsburg Trail 81

noisily at her temples. The door burst open and Kirsty, temporarily blinded by the sudden streak of sunlight slanting into the room, could only make out the man standing in the doorway as a vague, bulky, menacing shape. Plummer had a clearer, and for him, a more pleasurable and totally unexpected view. The blood-stirring sight of the Stoker girl dressed only in her drawers, proud young breasts on show. He stepped into the room grinning with lustful anticipation, already feeling the soft flesh under his hands. Kirsty's taut-nerves snapped and her finger jerked the trigger on the Colt in reflex action. Plummer's picture of paradise was blotted out by a pistol's flash and the acute pain of a bullet slicing the fleshy part of his upper left arm. He howled like a banshee and staggered back on to the porch holding his wounded arm.

Kirsty began breathing again, so fast and shallow with fear that her body shook as though racked by fever and the gun an almost unbearable weight in her hands. She laid the pistol down on the chair and as quickly as her trembling hands would allow her, slipped into her shift. Once more Kirsty picked up the pistol, re-cocked it, and holding it out at arm's length in front of her, forced her legs to walk the few, yet terrifying, paces to the door, fervently praying that her would-be rapist's cry of pain meant that the threat to her was over.

Garrett and Ben heard the shot as they cut across the farm on their way to Tularosa. They pulled up their horses and exchanged grim-faced looks.

'Could be trouble,' Garrett said. 'We'll ride....' He stopped: he was talking to himself. Ben was already rib-kicking his horse in the direction of the house. Damnit, he thought, the kid could be riding full tilt into an ambush. Then also opined that he would have gone mad-ass haring in twenty years ago if the girl he was fond of seemed in danger. He yanked his rifle out of his boot and heeling his horse into a gallop, followed in the wake of his deputy's trail-dust.

Kirsty stepped warily on to the porch, the tension within her one all-over body ache. She glimpsed a sudden movement to her left and wildly swung round trying to bring the pistol to bear on the hulking, black-whiskered man who sprang at her. She gave a sharp cry of pain as his pistol barrel struck her wrist causing her to drop the Colt to the porch floor from fingers that had numbly lost their grip. Then her attacker held his pistol against her head and pressed his body hard against her forcing her back up against the doorpost. His liquor-smelling breath and acrid body heat almost making her throw up.

'Me and you are goin' inside, missee,' Plummer mouthed. 'You're goin' to fix this arm you've winged. Then we're goin' to have some real fun. You've got plenty of time for you to make it good for me; there's no one about to interrupt us. Your kid brother heard the shot and tried to poke his nose in. I gave him a taste of this.' Plummer

Trouble on the Lordsburg Trail 83

waved the pistol in front of her eyes. 'He ain't hurt bad; I only knocked him cold for a spell.'

Looking past her captor Kirsty saw Jonathan lying in a small crumpled heap at the end of the porch. Worrying about her own safety she had forgotten about the danger Jonathan could be in. Mad angry, feeling that somehow she had let Jonathan down, Kirsty yelled, 'You dirty sonuvabitch!' and spat in Plummer's face and heedless of the pistol at her head attempted to knee Plummer in the groin.

Plummer cursed and cuffed her hard on the chin with the back of his pistol-holding fist. Kirsty gave a low moaning cry and fell against Plummer, almost passing out. He effortlessly gathered her up in his good arm and hoisted her over his shoulder, savouring the sweet softness he intended enjoying at his leisure, the taking of a high-spirited young virgin more satisfying to his taste than the simulated jerks and twists of a jaded two-dollar whore. His sap was too fully raised now to waste time having the wound on his arm seen to so Plummer carried his prize straight into the bedroom and flung her down on the bed, then began loosening his flies.

Kirsty's head cleared somewhat and when she saw what Plummer was doing made to get off the bed. Plummer cursed and pushed her back down and getting on the bed knelt across Kirsty's legs, pinning her tight between his thighs. He ripped off Kirsty's shift and with his teeth and one hand, tore it into strips. Kirsty screamed in her panic, arms thrashing as she fought back.

'I'm goin' to tie your hands to the bedposts,' Plummer grunted. 'I sure don't want you to tire yourself out before the fun starts.'

Plummer swung himself off the bed, breathing heavily, not only with the exertion of strapping down Kirsty's wildly flailing arms but with having a further taste of things to come. Kirsty ceased her futile screaming and kicking and lay back on the bed, physically and mentally drained. Plummer gave her a gloating horn-dog grin as he took in the sweat-sheened rising and falling breasts as Kirsty gasped for breath. With horror-filled eyes she watched Plummer as he began to strip off. The nightmare experience with her stepfther was about to be played again, this time to its fearful conclusion. Quietly she sobbed, wishing she were dead.

Ben heard her terrified screams as he closed in on the house. He yanked his mount to a sliding-haunched, dust-raising halt and leapt out of his saddle, both pistols drawn. He paused in his stride as he stepped on to the porch and saw Jonathan at the far end shakily pulling himself to his feet. Garrett, seeing a single horse standing outside the house, as he reined in behind Ben, called out, 'You go in, it looks as though there's only one of them, I'll see to the boy!'

Ben didn't give a damn if there was a whole army of the sons-of-bitches inside. Kirsty's screams and what she could be going through had worked him up so much that he would willingly go crashing through the gates of hell and take on the Devil himself to help her. It was as if somehow Kirsty had suddenly become real close kin to him. Yet his anger was cool and controlled. Both guns held steady and cocked, hard-lined faced, he continued on into the house.

Plummer, about to step out of his pants, heard the sound of running footsteps, spun round and saw Ben through the open doorway. He snatched for his pistol lying on a chair, an attempt he knew with terrible finality was as useless as the girl's struggles had been to stop him from using her. A detached part of his mind fleetingly fretted on the fact of how he could be feasting his eyes on the delights of a young girl's body one second then the next, looking at certain death from the pistols of Shorty's 'fast-shooting kid'.

Ben's first two shells put Plummer beyond fretting about anything at all for evermore. Firing from the living-room, first with the Navy, and then Pena's Dragoon, the shots spun Plummer round the end of the bed, feet tangled in his pants. Face stone-hard, Ben cut loose again with the right then the left pistol, hitting Plummer between the shoulders. Thrusting him away from the bed as though being pushed by invisible hands, an already dead man. The fifth and six shells caught Plummer as he was falling and sent him crashing into the bedroom window, breaking the frame and glass, ending up with arms and head hanging out over the porch.

Garrett, with a comforting arm round

Jonathan's shoulders, smiled with grim satisfaction as he heard the six regular spaced shots. An executioner's shots, the kid's shots. He sheathed his pistol and looked down at Jonathan. 'Let's go inside, Jonathan,' he said. 'Your sister may need our help.'

Ben put his own pistols away and walked into the bedroom, hardly daring to look at the bed. He had only seen the lower part of Kirsty's legs from the other room. He could have shouted out his relief to see that Kirsty wasn't completely naked, she still had her drawers on, only just, so he opined that the man he had the pleasure of shooting had not used her.

Kirsty looked at Ben with frightened, unbelieving eyes as he began loosening her bonds. He tried hard not to notice the well-rounded breasts brushing against his elbow as he leaned across her to reach her left wrist, not wishing to embarrass her anymore than she must be right now by having shown almost all she possessed to two men.

'Er, cover yourself up, Miss Kirsty,' Ben said, still not looking directly at her. 'I'll get rid of that scum.'

Kirsty sat on the edge of the bed and draped a sheet over her shoulders, still not fully comprehending that she was no longer in danger. Ben heaved Plummer clean through the window to land on the porch with a board-rattling thud. He had caused enough trouble in the house, Ben thought, without staining the carpet and floor with his blood.

Garrett came into the room on his own. He gave

Ben a 'good-job-done' nod then looked at Kirsty sitting white, drawn-faced on the bed. Quickly realizing that the state she was in – still in shock, near naked – that if wanting any comfort at all she would prefer it from an older, married man. Mr Howard being in the room was embarrassing her.

'Jonathan's in the other room, Deputy Howard,' Garrett said. 'Go and tell him his sister's OK.' He jerked his head in the direction of the door to chivvy Ben along if he didn't get the urgency of him moving from the tone of his voice.

Ben looked at him then across at Kirsty and guessed the reason for Garrett's command. 'I'll clear that fella off the porch as well, Mr Garrett,' he said and left the room.

'Jonathan!' cried Kirsty, coming alive and springing to her feet. 'Has he been harmed?'

Giving her a fatherly smile Garrett walked over to her. 'He's fine. He'll have a headache for the rest of the day that's all. It's you he's worried about.'

Kirsty gazed up at the tall man and all she was feeling inside loosened up and come bursting out in a flood of tears. Garrett held her close and gentle as a father would a frightened child.

'I, I haven't thanked Mr Howard for saving me from that man, Mr Garrett,' she sniffed between tears. 'But I couldn't I felt....' Kirsty's words ended in another burst of body-racking sobs.

'He'll understand how you were feeling, Miss Kirsty,' Garrett said soothingly. 'You're not rightly dressed for thanking young men, are you now? You go and make yourself pretty again and brew me and Mr Howard some of your fine coffee. Mr Howard will take that as a good enough thank you.' He kissed her on top of her head and let go of his hold on her.

'Thanks, Mr Garrett,' Kirsty said, smiling at him through her tears. 'I'll do as you say.' She would have liked to have given him a kiss in return but even if she stretched right up on her toes she could never reach Mr Garrett's face. And if she tried the sheet could slip off her shoulders. Kirsty could feel herself going all hot and cold again with embarrassment and without saying another word hurried out of the room.

Ben was sitting on the porch with Jonathan, trying to ease the pain the boy must be feeling from the knock on his head, by telling him he had true grit to go up against a gunman unarmed. He had to have a gun in each hand before he had the nerve to go in and face him. Garrett joined them on the porch and told Jonathan to go inside and let his sister see for herself that he wasn't hurt bad then he sat alongside Ben and got down to the serious business of discussing their next moves in the light of the attack on Kirsty.

'It proves that the sonsuvbitches haven't given up wanting to see me and Mr Chisum dead, Mr Howard,' Garrett said. 'And they knew that the farm would be the first place we would visit. So I did right to send Chisum north, out of danger, although the old goat wasn't too keen to go. Shorty must have seen my deputies before they left camp; that, I reckon, is why this time it was only one man. Kind of a one-man scouting party. I only hope that they still keep thinking that I've got my boys with me. Could make them a mite cautious, give us time to prepare ourselves. The sooner I show myself in town the easier life will be for the girl, they'll not need to look for me here. Though I think that you should stay the night at the farm. The girl's still naturally upset and trouble for her mightn't be over yet.'

He then proceeded to tell Ben that they should work independently in Tularosa. By taking the dead man in he would find out who he had ridden with, who bossed over them, enabling him to get an idea of the size of the opposition. 'Till we put them in Boot Hill or in the calaboose, we can't hope to get to Logan,' Garrett said finally.

'How do we put this gang where you want them?' a puzzled Ben asked. 'The only one of them we can lay charges against is the asshole who shot Betsy. And we've got to find him first.'

Garrett gave Ben a mirthless grin. 'It will be legal enough to shoot them down like mad dogs the next time they try to kill me. That's where you come in, Deputy Howard, you'll be watching my back. You'll ride into Tularosa as who you were when you crossed the Pegos – an innocent-looking backwoods boy on his way to Lordsburg to see his kinfolk. The only man who can finger you as a lawman is the one who stole your horse. Keep out of his way and no one will suspect that you're not what you seem to be. Oh, one thing more,' Garrett added. 'We'll have to ask the girl if we can borrow a horse and saddle off her, the mount you're riding is bound to be known in Tularosa. Men will notice that its real owner isn't up on its back and start asking you awkward questions.'

'It's kinda risky, don't you think, Mr Garrett, putting yourself up as a target?' Ben said, not too happy at knowing that he could be responsible for the tall lawman's life.

'It's no riskier than getting bushwhacked or shot in the back sitting at a campfire some dark night.' Garrett's smile suddenly showed genuine warmth. 'My way will give me a first-class *pistolero* looking out for me.' Becoming sober-faced again he said, 'And that's the Goddamned truth, Deputy Howard. I wouldn't be putting my life on the line otherwise. I'm fond of living as the next man.' He got to his feet. 'Let's get some of that coffee down us I can smell brewing then I can hit the trail to Tularosa.'

Kirsty put out the lights after she had seen Jonathan settled down in his bed. Mr Howard, on watch in the barn, had told her to act as she would normally do at night, the one exception being that he had asked her to hang a storm lantern on the porch near the door. Kirsty tried not to let her mind dwell too long on the reason Mr Howard wanted the porch lit up.

There was another exception to her usual nightly chores, one that Mr Howard didn't know

Trouble on the Lordsburg Trail 91

about. Although she was dog-tired she wasn't going to go to bed, knowing that the terrifying thoughts of what could have happened to her today, would cause many such sleepless nights before she could rest peacefully in bed once more. Even just looking at her bed started her shaking again. She piled more logs on the fire and sat down in a chair in front of it. It was going to be a long night. Kirsty smiled wanly. It had been one helluva day. But she had to live with it if she wanted to keep the farm going. She was glad that Mr Howard had said he would stay till morning, she wouldn't have stayed the night otherwise. It had been one helluva day for him also, she thought, he had killed a man and could have easily got himself killed.

While he and Mr Garrett had been drinking their coffee, and finding that her embarrassed annoyance at him seeing her almost naked was cooling, she had thanked him for coming to her aid at risk to his own well-being. After all, she had convinced herself, he hadn't burst into her bedroom just to gaze on her bared breasts, just as it wasn't her doing that they were bared. And it wasn't that she had seen him gloating over what he could obviously see. So why all the fuss and upset she was giving herself over events neither of them had control over? Kirsty found herself once more trying to answer the question of what on earth did it matter what Mr Howard may, or may not, think of her when, come morning, he would be riding out of her life.

Kirsty's hands flew to her mouth to stop a sudden realization. 'Good Lord,' she breathed in disbelief. Could her unexplained interest in what Mr Howard thought about her be because she *wanted* him to think about her? Was she growing fond of him? M'be she was falling in love with him. Kirsty gave another Good Lord gasp. She had never had a relationship with a boy before, didn't know how a girl fell in love with a boy, other than what she had read of it in magazines. The men in those stories were all tall and handsome, city-dressed, knew all about good food and fine wines. Swept the heroines off their dainty shod feet. Not some farm boy hardly bigger than her with a hole burnt in his jacket. Kirsty evoked the name of her Saviour again. The hole; she had promised him she would mend it for him. Though it hadn't been entirely her fault she hadn't repaired it. Mr Howard hadn't given the coat to her.

How could she be falling in love with a boy she had only met a few hours ago and had the cheek to cast sneering looks at her for the way she was dressed? It certainly didn't seem, Kirsty thought, that he was feeling the same way towards her. He was not much older than she was yet he had already killed, by what she had heard from the deputies, four men with his pistol. One of the men he had killed had been on her behalf. And he was out there, ready to kill again if needs be to protect her. 'Kirsty,' she said out loud, 'you're a blamed fool. You wouldn't know love if it came and hit you

Trouble on the Lordsburg Trail   93

in the eye.' Mr Howard was showing his feelings for her the only way he could, indeed had already shown them, by putting himself in front of her to protect her from harm.

Kirsty gave another lopsided smile. It wasn't like the magazine romances she had read at all. But as sure as hell, she thought, life to her these past years had been anything but romantic. Her mixed up thoughts and emotions about Mr Howard became a dull nagging pain in the pit of her stomach. As she dropped off into a fitful doze Kirsty wondered if it was romance why did it hurt so much?

As soon as he saw the lamps in the house go out, Ben, sitting on his bedroll just inside the barn, picked up his Winchester, worked the action, then laid it handy across his knees. Like his two pistols the long gun was fully loaded. By the light from the lantern he had a clear sighting of the porch door and well within easy rifle fire distance.

He accepted the fact that he wouldn't be getting much sleep, reckoned that it was a small price to pay if it kept Kirsty from any danger. He pictured again in his mind's eye the sight of her lying on the bed and thought what it would be like lying alongside her. Yet without a lewd thought in his mind. He was imagining being married to her and she being a willing, eager bed partner. And that, thought Ben, sarcastically, was real *loco* thinking. He had been as close to her, and seen more of her, as he ever would do. What future could she see for herself and Jonathan hitching up with him, if she by some miracle was so inclined, an almost broke, ragged-assed shootist? Ben's face twisted in a painful, lost-cause grin. Why, it took her all her time to smile at him. Though he had to admit that he was partly to blame for that by upsetting her the first time he had clapped his eyes on her. He cleared his head of such fanciful thoughts and concentrated on the serious task in hand. To blow to hell, or wherever, any other son-of-a-bitch who came to harm Kirsty.

NINE

The night life in Tularosa had almost died away when Garrett, rope-leading the horse with its former owner a tarp-wrapped bundle on its back, rode into town. Apart from a few drunks staggering noisily along the boardwalks, Main Street was quiet. An emptiness which suited Garrett. It gave him undisturbed time to find out what he and his deputy were taking on.

He dismounted outside the town jail and tied both horses to the hitching rail. The place was in darkness but Garrett was banking on at least one deputy being inside, to see to the wants of any prisoners occupying the cells, drunks and suchlike, if the sheriff was out doing his nightly rounds. Someone he hoped, who could identify the dead man and who he ran with. Equally important, to be told not to break the news of Pat Garrett being in Tularosa till daybreak. By then the slick-shooting Mr Howard would be on his way in to even up the odds they could be facing.

Garrett untied the body from the horse and slung it over his shoulder and stepping up to the jailhouse door rapped loudly on it. After a while he heard the sounds of bolts being drawn and someone not too happy at being woken up swearing and cursing a blue streak. Garrett grinned, thinking that if a fella can't stand the pace then he shouldn't wear the badge. The door swung open, the light from the held lantern momentarily blinding him, so he couldn't see the man who said in a drunk's slurred voice, 'What the hell's the trouble? Can't it wait?' Sheriff Paxton held the lantern higher with a hand that shook as much as his voice had. 'Holy shit,' he croaked as he took in more of the tall figure of Garrett and the bundle he had across his left shoulder. 'Who the hell's that you're totin'?'

'I'm hoping you'll tell me that, Paxton,' replied Garrett, roughly elbowing Paxton aside and entering the jail house.

'You're way out of your jurisdiction, Garrett,' Paxton protested, trying to put some of the authority that came with the tin-star in his voice.

Garrett saw a big man, running to fat, unshaven, shirt hanging loose over his big belly and smelling like a moonshiner's still. If he hadn't known him as a fellow peace officer he would have labelled him as the town drunk earning his liquor money by keeping the jail house clean. Garrett gave him a cutting look as with one hand he swept the office desk clear of its papers, left-over food and whiskey bottle, and laid the dead man across it.

'We'll leave the finer points of my jurisdiction till later, Sheriff,' Garrett said curtly. Spitting the word 'sheriff' out as though he had said 'shit'. 'You just take a look at this pilgrim and tell me who he is and who his buddies are?'

Paxton bent low and holding the lantern over the body, turned down a corner of the tarp. 'Why it's Plummer,' he said. Straightening up he looked at Garrett. 'He was long due for being wrapped up the way he is.'

'So, who are his pals?' asked Garrett. 'And where do they hang out?'

'That ain't your concern, Garrett,' Paxton blustered. 'I'm the law around here.' Putting the lamp down on the desk he began to tuck his shirt back down his pants in a forlorn effort to regain some of his liquor-drowned pride.

'I know Tularosa isn't my town, Sheriff,' Garrett said conversationally. 'But I'll tell you this, if you don't co-operate with me I'll send a wire to Mr Chisum who will have words with his good friend, Governor Wallace, about how that asshole who wears the lawman's badge in Tularosa lets men who attempt to rape a young girl, and try to murder a leading citizen in the territory, Mr John Chisum himself, run around free in his town. Then there'll be state marshals running the law around here in no time at all and you'll be back where you belong, swamping in some bar.'

'Did Plummer try to do that?' asked an amazed Paxton, ignoring Garrett's insults.

Garrett's face creased in an ice-cold grin. 'There were three other *hombres* involved, we buried two of them but the third, a fella called Shorty, took off on a stolen horse. I reckon he comes within my jurisdiction. A horse-thief can be legally shot or hanged by anyone who catches up with him. Now is Plummer here with the same bunch as Shorty and the two we killed? A Mex cutthroat named Pena was one of them, so who runs them and how many like-minded sonsuvbitches does he have?'

'Pena?' said a surprised Paxton. 'How the hell did you sneak up on him?'

Garrett favoured Paxton with his mirthless smile once more. 'He got careless, underestimated a young kid.'

'He was Kerney's right-hand man,' said Paxton. 'Plummer, and I reckon the other fella you shot, were two of his gang, likewise Shorty, though come to think of it I ain't seen him in the White Sands saloon the past day or so.'

'And what line of business is this Mr Kerney in, Sheriff?' asked Garrett. 'And where can he be found, and what does he look like?'

'Kerney runs a small bunch of men,' Paxton replied. 'Moves cattle and suchlike activities for Mr Logan, you'll know of his spread.' Garrett nodded. 'Kerney generally hangs out in the White Sands when he's in town,' continued Paxton. 'He's a little fella, mean-eyed.' Paxton forced a weak grin. 'Most of his boys favour that kinda look. Though Kerney's handsome looks ain't improved any by a knife scar running down his left cheek.'

'I don't suppose this mean-eyed Mr Kerney is too fussy about bills of sales for the cattle he moves around,' Garrett said.

Trouble on the Lordsburg Trail 99

'Now there ain't any proof that Kerney's in the cattle-liftin' trade, Mr Garrett,' Paxton said with new-found belligerency in his voice. 'If there was I'd run him in.'

Garrett felt like telling Paxton that the state he was in he couldn't run himself to the crapper but not wanting to upset the old soak more than he had done already by coming into his town, and needing his help, he said, 'There'll be proof enough to hang Kerney and his boys before I leave Tularosa.' He hard-eyed Paxton. 'Outside my bailiwick or not. Now, I'd like to borrow a riot gun and a box of reloads from your armoury; I'll sign for them, then I'll go and book a room for myself in the Wades Hotel. You can see to Plummer and his effects.'

After Garrett had left, Sheriff Paxton slumped down heavily in his chair and gave Plummer's corpse a sour-eyed look. He picked up the whiskey bottle and took several long, nerve-soothing gulps. Big trouble was about to hit Tularosa, he thought, and he wanted no part in it, drunk or sober.

TEN

Ben suddenly came awake when he felt his arm being shaken and made a grab for the Winchester. Then he saw frightened-faced Jonathan jumping back from bending over him.

'You did tell me to wake you after you'd been asleep a couple of hours, Mr Howard,' said Jonathan apprehensively.

Ben smiled at him as he sat up on the bales of straw. 'I did that, Jonathan,' he said. 'I'm sorry I threw a scare into you, but I'm kinda scared myself. The last few days ain't exactly been the most peaceful and joyous days I've spent.'

'Sis says to tell you that there's coffee and hot food ready if you want to eat before you ride out,' Jonathan said.

'I sure do,' Ben replied. 'Though I'll wash up before I come in.' Ben had intended riding out from the farm a little after dawn but hadn't been too happy about leaving Kirsty so soon. There had been no alarms raised during the night but that didn't mean the sons-of-bitches had given up, and there could be more than one this time. He weighed that possibility with Garrett in Tularosa

Trouble on the Lordsburg Trail 101

relying on him to watch his back. Thinking things through he couldn't see Garrett being in any immediate danger from the gang or whatever the three dead men belonged to just yet. Garrett would have arrived in Tularosa too late for the news of his presence in the town to have circulated around the saloons and bars. If there was going to be a move against the lawman, he opined, it would come tonight, during the dark hours. A further reason for him deciding to stay longer at the farm was that he needed a few hours' sleep. Ben grinned inwardly. A tired *pistolero* would be no damned good to Garrett if he got himself in a tight corner. Hoping that his reasoning was sound he gave his face a quick splashing of cold water from the trough to bring him fully awake, dried himself, then walked on into the house.

Kirsty, holding Jonathan's hand, stood on the porch to watch Ben ride off. She wished him good luck then impetuously kissed him lightly on the cheek before he mounted up.

'I'll see that you get the horse and saddle back, Miss Kirsty,' Ben said. 'Mr Garrett will be riding this way again when he heads back to Lincoln so I don't think he'll mind being burdened with an extra horse for a short spell.' With a farewell touch of his hat he heeled his mount into a gentle canter.

'Why didn't you ask Mr Howard to come back, Sis?' Jonthan said. 'I think you were hoping he'd come back with the horse.'

Kirsty took her gaze off the soon to be riding out

of her sight, and life, Ben, and looked down at her brother. How could a young boy know what was going on inside her? Was it so obvious in her face? She had wanted him to come back. She was in no doubt now that she was in love with him. She had been frightened to ask him in case he had turned down her plea. In love with Mr Howard or not, she still had her pride. She thin-smiled Jonathan.

'Now why would Mr Howard want to pay us a second visit, Jonathan, if I did ask him to? He's on his way to Lordsburg to live with his kinfolk. Rode all the way from the Nations to see them. He can't waste any more of his time calling on two out-of-the-way sodbusters, can he Jonathan? Now let's go inside and get on with our chores; we've a farm to run, remember?' What Kirsty really wanted was some quiet corner out of the way of Jonathan where she could bawl her eyes out like some kid for allowing her stubborn-mule pride to come before the chance of possible happiness for her and Jonathan.

Ben looked over his shoulder once and gave them a final goodbye wave before a dip in the trail cut them from his sight. He wasn't too disappointed in the manner of his leaving. He reckoned that Kirsty could see nothing in him to want to clutch at his legs and beg him to come back to the farm. He smiled, an effort no deeper than Kirsty's had been. He had got a kiss from her, more than he expected. Even if he had been asked he couldn't have promised to pay them another visit. He didn't know how much trouble lay ahead of him.

Could be the next riding he would be doing would be in an undertaker's hearse to Boot Hill. All appearance of his smile vanished from his face as he urged his horse into a gallop, to widen the distance between him and how things might have been.

ELEVEN

Garrett sat on the porch of the White Sands saloon, the shotgun resting across his knees, a silent but ominous message to anyone who cared to read it that Sheriff Pat Garrett wasn't just sitting on his ass in the shade to escape the baking noon heat. He had come to Tularosa on lawman's business, killing business if warranted.

The hard-drinking men were already drifting into the White Sands, Garrett close-eyeing them from under the brim of his forward-tilted hat. To his jaundiced gaze they all seemed to have owlhoots' pinched-assed visages. That, he opined, would make the likely number of men Kerney had riding for him the equivalent of a whole company of horse soldiers. and he had yet to see the man with the scar on his cheek, the bossman, Kerney.

Garrett began to worry about Ben still not showing up. Began to wonder if he had been too late in openly showing himself in Tularosa. Too late for Logan to call off his wolves from seeking him and Chisum at the Stoker farm. Mr Howard could be fighting a real battle while he was sitting here trying to figure out who were the bad guys.

It was a much relieved Garrett who watched Ben come slow-riding along Main Street. As he rode past him Ben gave a slight nod and he took that to mean that everything was OK at the farm. He noticed that his deputy wasn't wearing a gunbelt, living up to his image as a backwoods boy aimlessly drifting through the territory. Garrett smiled. Some asshole would get to wondering on his way to hell how the kid whom he had the drop on, brought a gun he hadn't known he'd had into play so quick.

Ben, after stabling his horse, followed Garrett's instructions and booked a room in Wade's Hotel. He thought that he would have time to buy himself the new coat with money Chisum had left with Garrett to honour his promise before the lawman contacted him to bring up to date on how things were shaping up for them.

Ben stood gallantly aside to allow two girls to come out of the draper's. They were girls with heavily made-up faces and their dresses even shorter than the one Kirsty had worn. The pair of them smiled and bold-eyed him. The nearest, a dark-haired girl, edged real close to him till he could feel the heat from her thighs through the material of her dress. He coloured up, embarrassed, causing the girl to giggle. Suddenly his temperature dropped and his eyes widened in surprise. The other girl, a blonde, was wearing his ma's necklace.

Only half listening, Ben heard the girl pressing herself against him say, 'You seem a stranger in town; are you going to pay me and Pearl here, a visit? We work in the Sporting House, just down the street there. We'll see to it that you remember your trip to Tularosa. Won't we, Pearl?'

Pearl favoured Ben with a big, skin-deep, working-girl's smile. 'We sure will, Flo, he'll think Christmas has come early this year.' Both girls broke into a fit of giggling.

Ben somehow controlled his anger on seeing a whore wearing one of his ma's treasured mementoes. He knew who she must have got the necklace from but he couldn't start asking her questions about Shorty's whereabouts out here in the street. More than likely the hard-faced Pearl would tell him it was no business of his who gave the necklace to her, could tell him to get lost. And he could do damn all about it, unless he wanted a stand-up row with her. Then his link with Shorty would be known and Garrett would lose the only edge he had, a pardner the opposition didn't know about.

Ben gave a moon-faced, eager-eyed smirk. 'Ah sure am goin' tuh pay yuh a visit, little lady. Why ah'm as horny as a hound dog in heat. Ah tell a lie, little lady, ah'm as randy as two hound dogs.' He linked arms with the girls, his smirk now a lecherous leer. 'Yuh two purty ladies lead me tuh that paradise of yours, ah'm rarin' to go.'

Garrett sat up straight in his chair in surprised disappointment on seeing his deputy arm in arm with the whores. Had he read the kid wrong as a steady, sensible-minded boy, reliable in a crisis? Opined that he had strong feelings for a fine girl like Kirsty? Yet there he was acting like some trail-hand at the end of a six-week drive. The fast *pistolero* had let him down. He had crawled out on a limb and there was no one to prevent any son-of-a-bitch sawing it off behind him. Garrett gripped the shotgun tighter, watched the men going into the saloon closer. If any of them gave him more than a cursory curious glance he would have to tag them as members of the Kerney gang and watch them like hawks or Billy the Kid would have to forego the pleasure of killing him.

Ben paused on the stone steps of the Sporting House, let go of Pearl's arm and took off his hat, and looking over his shoulder in the direction of Garrett, wiped his brow with the sleeve of his coat. 'Ah do declare,' he grinned. 'Yuh ladies are raisin' mah sweat already.' Then he continued on into the cathouse. Hoping that Garrett would make sense out of his signal.

A slow smile brightened up Garrett's dour face. 'Why you young son-of-a-bitch,' he breathed, 'you've got yourself a lead. I didn't misjudge you after all.' He sat back in the chair as relaxed as any man could be contemplating that he could be forced into a gunfight in the not-too-distant future. And he suddenly discovered how much he depended on Deputy Ben Howard. Pat, he thought, you're getting too long in the tooth for this kind of caper.

'Do you want me to start taking my clothes off now?' Pearl said. 'Or are you gonna wait till Flo comes up with the whiskey? Pearl, sitting on the edge of the bed, looked up questioningly at Ben standing facing the room door. Pearl was rapidly calculating how many glasses of the firewater that passed for drinking-man's whiskey in the Sporting House the kid would down before he didn't know, or care, a hoot, if he was still in the State of New Mexico or dancing ballicky-naked in Timbucto. And when she and Flo dragged him down the stairs and dumped him in the back alley she reckoned, from past experiences, when the kid came round he wouldn't know if he had done all the things he said he was going to do on finding himself broke. If he did feel sore about waking up in an alley instead of a nice soft bed pressed against a girl then it would be their word against a violently drunk kid who had to be thrown out before he wrecked the place and harmed the girls.

Conscious that Garrett was out there waiting for his backup Ben fretted impatiently for Flo to come up with the drinks. He wanted both girls in the room so that he could threaten the pair of them with jail for being involved in the handling of stolen jewellery if they put it around that he was interested in putting Shorty, and the man who gave him his orders, behind bars. He didn't know, being only a temporary deputy, if he had the authority to jail the girls but he was relying on them being as ignorant of the law as he was.

To get both girls into the room, Ben, on entering the porch of the cathouse, had stretched his acting role as a genuine horn dog looking for a good time. 'Ah'm hopin' the two of yuh are goin' tuh entertain me,' he had said. 'Ah ain't hard-assed all the way tuh this fair city of yours just tuh fool around. Ah'm cravin' real excitement.'

'My, my,' Flo said. 'We've netted ourselves a real curly wolf, Pearl.' Sharp-eyeing Ben she added, 'Can you pay for two of us? Special sessions cost extra.'

Ben waved his arms magnanimously. 'Ah'm loaded. Just sold mah holdin', cash on the barrel-head.' He put his hand into his coat pocket and showed Flo a fist full of silver dollars, his new coat money. 'This is only the small change, honey. You name your price and ah'll settle up with yuh upstairs. If the pair of yuh are good tuh me' – he gave a leering horny wink – 'why ah'll see that yuh get something extra for your sweet selves.'

Flo quickly convinced herself that the horny kid could pay for his extra pleasures though he didn't dress like a man with a lot of spending money. But appearances, as she well knew, and money didn't always go together. She had entertained snappy-dressed, smooth-talking *hombres* who hadn't two red cents to rub together. Yet she had been humped by an old gold prospector, dressed in goat skins and stinking like one, who shook out enough gold dust out of his clothes in his haste to get stripped off to almost pay for his session.

'OK, then,' she said, 'you've got yourself a ball, mister. Now ain't it about time you told us your name, you know ours?'

'Ben Howard,' Ben said, giving her the full treatment of his village idiot's grin once more.

'OK, Ben,' said Flo. 'You go upstairs with Pearl, I'll go and order some drinks then the three of us can have a real humdinger of a ball.'

'I said do you want me to take my clothes off now, Ben?' repeated Pearl, beginning to guess that now the moment had come the kid was chickening out, showing himself to be nothing but a blowhard who had probably never been with a woman before. An easy mark – if they played it right. Keep pouring the whiskey down Mr Howard's neck, then taking their clothes off would be the only work she and Flo would have to do. No sweat, no pain. Like money from home.

Ben gave her a hard-eyed look. 'For starters you can take off that necklace,' he grated. 'Like the rest of the jewellery you've just come by, it doesn't belong to you.'

Pearl's jaw dropped open with surprise at the sudden change in her client's character. Gone were the big stupid grin and the hillbilly drawl. 'What do you mean, they don't belong to me?' she cried angrily but uneasily at the same time. 'A very good friend gave the pieces to me as a present.'

'Your good friend, Shorty, is a no-good horse-thief who I intend seeing strung up, if I don't shoot him dead myself. Along with stealing my horse he stole the jewellery you've got; it was my ma's. The sonuvabitch was in with them who tried to kill Mr Chisum. So your good friend ain't got no good in him at all. While you're handing over the jewellery you can tell me where Shorty's hiding out and who the man is he works for.'

Pearl, determined to hang on to what she thought was rightly hers, told Ben what he could do in words he had never thought a female would use, leastways not in his hearing.

Ben sighed resignedly. 'I hoped that it would not come to this, hoped that you would see reason, so we'll have to do it the hard way. You and me will take a stroll along to the sheriff's office and let him decide who the jewellery belongs to.' He pulled out his deputy's badge from his shirt pocket and showed it to the glowering-eyed Pearl. 'I reckon he'll take the word of another lawman against the say-so of a two-dollar whore whose good friend is a common horse-thief. You could end up doing a stretch in the county jail for handling stolen property.'

Ben watched Pearl's face for her reactions to the situation he had put her in, hoping that his threat would work. The last thing he wanted was the sheriff to know the reason for him being in Tularosa, remembering Garrett saying that the lcoal lawman was one of Logan's appointees.

Flo came into the room while Pearl was still thinking through her options. 'We're ready for that ball,' she said and, broad-smiling, she laid down the tray of drinks on a table. Her smile thinned then faded away completely as she noticed the looks on Pearl's and Mr Howard's faces. A wave of sickening panic swept up from her stomach to the back of her throat. Had she and Pearl landed a *mal hombre*? A crazy guy who got his kicks by hurting the girls he used? A dreaded fear that all in her profession lived with. She knew of a girl whose face had been disfigured for life by a knife-wielding crazy.

Ben's face softened somewhat on seeing the fear mirrored in Flo's eyes. 'I'm not going to harm either of you so there's no need to be scared. Me and Pearl have just been having a friendly talk about some items she has which really belong to me.' He then told Flo the whole story.

When he had finished Flo glared angrily at Pearl. 'Give Mr Howard back his ma's jewellery you little fool!' she snapped. 'You oughta know that an asshole like Shorty don't come by anything he's got honestly. Get the rest of them out of your drawer and hand them to Mr Howard before you land yourself deeper in the shit than you are already.' Flo switched her gaze back on to Ben. 'Shorty earns his keep working for a fella named Kerney, Mr Howard. Shorty ain't no angel, as you already know, but compared to that sonuvabitch, Kerney, he's St Peter himself. Kerney and the rest of the boys who ride with him hang out, when they're not out robbing some poor innocent folk, in the White Sands saloon. Though Shorty won't be there. I've heard that he's lying low in a line cabin along the West Ridge trail.' She favoured Ben with the ghost of a smile. 'I reckon he knows you're huntin' him. If you're open to advice, Mr Howard, I'd watch out very carefully if you meet up with Kerney; as I said, he's one mean *hombre*. Now give Mr Howard his ma's jewellery, Pearl, so he can go about his business.' Suddenly Flo gave Ben a genuine, deep-feeling smile. 'Unless he still wants to stay and have that ball we promised him.'

'I would stay but for two reasons,' Ben said. 'One, there's a friend of mine out on the street waiting for me to back him up in some trouble he's stirring up.' He grinned at Flo. 'Secondly, you girls scare the hell outa me, and that's the truth. No offence intended to the pair of you but I'd be more comfortable facing this fella Kerney.' He then handed over all his new coat money to Flo. 'That should pay for the drinks and your wasted time. But I'll expect you to say nothing to anyone about what I've told you or me and my friend's necks could be at risk more than they are right now.'

Flo looked Ben straight in the eyes. 'Mr Howard,' she said, 'if we girls loose-mouthed only part of what we hear in these rooms half the wives in Tularosa would be hauled up in front of a judge for murdering their husbands for defamation of character.' She moved closer to Ben and kissed him on the mouth. 'It's a pity you ain't staying, and that's the truth as well. But you remember what I said about Kerney. Don't give him an inch; use that big pistol you've got stuck in the top of your pants if he so much as breaks wind.'

'I intend doing just that, Flo,' replied Ben grimly. A still not-too-happy-looking Pearl handed him the cloth-wrapped pieces of jewellery. Ben touched his hat to both girls. 'It's been a pleasure meeting you,' he said. 'I'm sorry for things not turning out for you as you expected, but they've sure never turned out the way I expected when I set off to ride to Lordsburg.'

Garrett got to his feet on seeing Ben leave the cathouse and stepping off the porch began strolling casually along the street, away from the saloon section. Ben, keeping on his side of Main Street, shadowed him. Garrett crossed over to his side and entered a dead-end alley that opened on to a boarded-up empty lot, Garrett waited in the deserted yard for his deputy to join him. Ben gave the street a quick up-and-down glance and, satisfied that no prying eyes were watching him, he slipped into the alley. Garrett gave him a grin when he came up to him.

'You had me worried for a moment, Deputy, when I saw you with those two ladies,' he said. 'Did you dig anything up?'

'I know where Shorty is,' replied Ben. 'I reckon by now you know who he and the man you brought in work for, and where they rest up when they're in town.'

Garrett nodded. 'I haven't seen Kerney yet but a bunch of his boys were in the saloon.' He grinned. 'I went inside and showed them my coat-tails. To let them know that I'm not in Tularosa just to pass the time of day with them. They'll know now that it's war.'

He had walked straight up to the bar and ordered a drink. With the shotgun resting easy in the crook of his left arm he surveyed the rest of the saloon's customers through the big flyblown mirror at the rear of the bar. He had noticed six men playing cards at a table to his left when he pushed through the doors; now they had stopped, devoting all their attention on him, easing chairs slightly away from the table to be able to get at pistols that much quicker.

Garrett saw pinched-assed looks on some of the other customers' faces as well. He put that down to the natural nervousness of men suddenly realizing that they could have landed in the middle of a shoot-out when they had only come in the saloon for a quiet drink and a game of cards. But six men, all at one table, giving him hard-eyed glares was too much of a coincidence. They could only be part of Kerney's gang. Though, disappointingly, he couldn't see one of the sons-of-bitches with a scar on his face.

Just to show them, if they didn't already know, how things could turn out for them if they tried something more harmful to him than drop-dead looks, he drew back the hammers of the shotgun. The twin ominous clicks made the barkeep almost drop the glass he was polishing and an expression came on his face as though he had just been caught short. His pointed gesture worked, the six men sat rigid on their chairs. Garrett finished his drink and turned away from the bar. With the shotgun now resting in the bend of his right arm loosely covering the six men, he walked out of the saloon and sat down on the porch chair again. Behind the swinging shut doors he heard the saloon come to life once more.

'You'd better go and see them for yourself, Deputy,' Garrett said. 'Then you'll be familiar with their ugly mugs, be able to keep tabs on them. That way we'll still have the edge over them. Kerney wasn't in the saloon. I'm told he has a knife scar on his face. So he shouldn't be hard to pick out of a crowd. Now what about the whereabouts of Mr Shorty?'

'He's shacked up in a line cabin along the west trail,' Ben said. 'He left Ma's jewellery with one of the girls you saw me with. She was wearing Ma's necklace, so I pretended that I wanted, well, you know what, Mr Garrett. Once inside I managed to persuade her that the jewellery really belonged to me and she gave it back to me.'

'That's good,' Garrett said. 'You haven't lost your reason for going on to Lordsburg; you can still honour your ma's wish.' He grinned. 'Now, I reckon, you're hankerin' to make a surprise call on Shorty.'

'Something like that,' replied Ben. 'If it don't interfere with what plans you've made regarding Kerney's gang.'

'I haven't made any plans,' Garrett said. 'Other than what we intended doing by coming to Tularosa, to draw any further trouble from Miss Kirsty, and take on the bastards on their own ground when they decide to move against us. So there's time for us to go and round up Shorty while that bunch in the saloon is sweating their balls off wondering what Pat Garrett's next moves are. Three of their buddies dead is bound to unsettle them. If we pull in Shorty that could make Kerney move sooner than later, m'be make him careless. I'll find out how far this line cabin is from town. Kerney could start something tonight and we don't want him to catch us in the dark riding along an unfamiliar trail. You go and take a look inside the saloon. I'll see you in half an hour or so along the west trail.'

Ben ordered a whiskey when he stepped up to the bar, not wanting to cause the same kind of trouble the asking of a soda pop had in Kingsville. Between forced sips of the fiery liquor Ben eyed the table Garrett had told him about. There were still six men sitting at it, none of them with a scar on their faces. So he took it that Kerney still hadn't yet showed up.

One of the men, black-whiskered, scowling-faced, like the man he had killed at the farm, gave him a look then carried on talking to his companions. He was too far away from the table to make out what the man was talking about above the general noise of the saloon but by the animated working of his face the black-whiskered man was discussing something more serious than an inquest on the card game they had just played. They were; the gang were arguing among themselves which was the best way to get Garrett off their backs.

Bud, the bearded man, firmly believed that they should have followed Garrett out of the saloon and shot him down in the street, avenging the deaths of Pena, Leroy and now Plummer. Cass, a narrow-faced man, who had difficulty holding his shifty-eyed gaze on anyone he happened to be talking to for more than a few seconds at a time just as firmly disagreed.

'And we would have all been as dead as them,' he said. 'That's what the bastard wanted us to do, follow him out and draw on him, then we would have been blown off the porch.'

'How do you make that out?' Bud growled truculently. 'He's good, I'll say that for him, but he ain't good enough to beat off the whole six of us. Why we'd cut him to pieces between us.'

'Yeah, he's good all right,' said Cass. 'But he ain't *loco*. He ain't come strolling in here just to invite us to shoot him down. Where do you think the three deputies and the fast-draw kid are that Shorty told Kerney about, eh? You can bet the next pot you win that they're skulking outside somewhere close for Garrett to lead us out to them. Garrett's putting himself up as a Judas goat but I ain't bitin'.'

'What Cass says makes sense, Bud,' another one of the gang said. 'Going mad-assed after Garrett would be like you playing a hand of cards blind.'

Bud dirty-mouthed Garrett, his deputies and the unknown kid for several minutes then asked them if they were just going to sit on their butts and let Garrett make all the moves.

Cass pushed back his chair and stood up. 'I ain't for one, Bud, but I ain't going off at half-cock. I'm

Trouble on the Lordsburg Trail 119

due to take some rations out to Shorty but I ain't takin' him any. I'm gonna tell him, bein' that he's the only one of us, who's still livin', has seen the kid and the deputies he's to haul ass and come back with me to town. Then I intend dragging him round every saloon in town till he spots Garrett's boys.' He favoured Bud with his wandering-eyed gaze. 'Then we can take them on, Bud, on equal terms and keep ourselves above ground.'

Ben waited a long minute when he saw one of Kerney's men walk out of the saloon. He decided against finishing off his drink to make everything appear normal, opining that he would need all his senses working at full blast if he was to find out where the man was bound for. He cast another quick look at the men at the table but didn't notice any of them eyeing him with suspicious interest so he left the bar to catch up with the man he was going to trail. Ben saw him go into the livery barn, then come out again mounted up, to head out of town by way, of what Ben reckoned, was the lie of the sun, the west trail. He thin-smiled. If his and Garrett's luck still held out, Kerney was set to lose two more of his gang.

Garrett saw the dust of a rider approaching from the direction of Tularosa and, gun-wise, he backed his mount deeper into the brush at the side of the trail. He recognized the rider as one of the six men he had seen in the saloon. Like his deputy he reckoned that they were about to win another round in the fight to expose Logan as a cattle-thief and a man who had put a killing price on Mr Chisum's head. The next rider along the trail was his deputy and Garrett nosed his horse out of the brush to greet him. He grinned. 'It looks as though we're flushing them out, Deputy. I reckon that there's no need for us to ride on any further, this seems a likely spot to pay our respects to the pair of them on their way back.'

TWELVE

Kerney had a lot troubling him: another one of his boys dead; Garrett roaming the town like a fighting dog looking for a battle; knowing that it was his boys who had tried to kill him and Chisum the battle was going to be between him and Garrett. He didn't need to be paid to kill Garrett. It was personal now; he had to down the son-of-a-bitch before he did likewise. If only he knew where the kid was who had done the fancy pistol work on Pena and Leroy he would be a lot more confident of getting the better of Garrett.

He had heard nothing about Garrett bringing in the dead Plummer. After an all-night, heavy drinking and poker session that had kept him sleeping it off till almost noon he had been on his way to the White Sands saloon for several glasses of the hair-of-the-dog and to find out if Plummer had returned with any news of Garrett's camp. Spicer had stopped him before he had made it to the saloon, telling him that Logan wanted to see him urgently, like now, before he wore holes in the carpet waiting for him.

Spicer grinned. 'You don't look fit enough to

climb up on to your horse let alone ride it as far as Sandy Creek. But you don't have to, the boss is waiting for you in his room at the Plains View Hotel, though he said that you had to come in by the back way.'

Jesus, thought Kerney, as he walked over to the hotel, somehow Logan must have heard that his attempt to kill Chisum and Garrett had been a balls up and wanted his down payment back. Why else would he want to see him here in Tularosa instead of out of town? Kerney gave a sick-gutted smile. Logan would be lucky, Kerney had lost a big chunk of the money hitting a bad streak of luck at poker last night.

Logan, pacing to and fro in his room like a caged mountain cat, was naturally put out somewhat on hearing the news that one of the men he had paid out good money to see dead had ridden into Tularosa last night, bringing with him the body of a man who worked for Kerney. Kerney, the son-of-a-bitch, had let him down, he thought, as he chewed savagely at the end of his cigar. Then, from a business standpoint, he reviewed his position. Though he would have dearly liked Chisum dead, it had been for personal reasons only. Chisum alive didn't stop him from building up his cattle empire. Garrett above ground was a different matter, a real threat to his hopes and aims. He was a lawman, a born snooper. He would soon link up Plummer with Kerney.

Whatever else Garrett was, he was a persistent bastard. He would pile the pressure on Kerney, close in on him, kill his boys when he could. Now he had to consider the possibility that to save his dirty hide, Kerney might talk and Chisum would get the proof he needed to pull him down. Kerney would have to be watched. His death could come earlier than he had planned it to happen. But getting back to business, the killing of Garrett could be postponed for a day or two. There was a more urgent problem he wanted Kerney to deal with.

Though Stoker was dead he still needed his land and he didn't know if Stoker's stepdaughter would be as co-operative as he had been. Billy was due with another bunch of longhorns and with Garrett and Chisum hanging around Tularosa it would be dangerous for Billy to be driving the herd any longer than he had to. For his and Billy's sake Stoker's stepdaughter would have to be persuaded to leave her farm, like quickly.

Kerney knocked on the door of Logan's private room and was barked at to come in. Kerney took the bull by the horns by telling the rancher why he had failed to kill Chisum and Garrett and of the shooting down of two of his men. 'But I've got another man scouting for their camp,' he said. 'As soon as he reports in I'll take all my boys out. So there should be no slip-up this time, we know about the kid now.'

'You don't know, do you, Kerney?' Logan said, incredulously.

'Know what, Mr Logan?' asked a still liquored brain-fuddled Kerney.

'Did you send Plummer out?' Logan said.

'Yeah, I did,' replied Kerney, getting more puzzled by the second. 'But what has that got to do with me not knowin' and what ain't I not knowin'?'

'What you're not knowing is that Garrett came into town last night with Plummer laid across his horse, stone cold dead, that's all.' Logan almost snarled his words out. 'Where the hell were you when this was happening? On another planet? Garrett, the sonuvabitch, is prowling around town as though he was the law here.'

'I'd a kinda heavy night,' Kerney mumbled.

Logan gave him a withering look and started his pacing again, silent-tongued. He stopped and faced Kerney. 'And who the hell is this kid, you mentioned?' he asked. 'What's he got to do with Garrett? Is he one of his deputies?'

'I don't know, Mr Logan,' replied Kerney. 'He was with Garrett and Chisum at their camp when my boys jumped them. What I do know is he's fast with a gun. I mean real slick. Shorty told me the kid gunned down Pena and Leroy while they had the drop on him. So you see why I had to be cautious before I went up against Garrett again. That's why I sent Plummer to check things out.'

'Damn all good it did too, didn't it?' Logan snarled. He saw Kerney's face twist in anger and for one panicky moment he thought he had pushed Kerney too far; he didn't want him to quit on him, his work wasn't done yet. And as sure as hell he didn't want the murdering son-of-a-bitch

Trouble on the Lordsburg Trail 125

to feel that mad-angry against him to pull out his gun and plug him. Voice mollified somewhat he said, 'OK, OK, so your boys came up against something they didn't count on till it was too late for them to do anything about it. But that's past history now. That don't mean I don't want Garrett dead – you can forget about Chisum – and I want no slip up next time, even if the son-of-a-bitch has a dozen fast gun kids with him, or I'll have to reconsider the financial arrangement I made with you, savvy? But before seeing to Garrett I want Stoker's stepdaugher off her land. Let her put her bits and pieces on a wagon then burn her place down, and I don't want her harmed.'

Logan hadn't suddenly developed a caring conscience and didn't want to see a young girl hurt, m'be killed. He wouldn't care a damn hurting his own mother, if she stood in his way. The harming of an orphan girl would get Tularosa a bad name and Governor Lew Wallace could declare martial law in Tularosa as he had done in Lincoln. Blue-belly soldier boys would then be administrating the law here putting his and Billy the Kid's cattle dealings out of business. 'Do you think that you and your boys can handle the girl?' he said, having a last malicious dig at Kerney.

Only the fact that he wouldn't get away with it prevented Kerney from pulling out his knife and giving Logan a taste of what he had given Stoker. So instead he ate crow and said, 'If Garrett ain't watching us we'll have the girl on her way by nightfall.'

'I'll expect to hear from you tomorrow that that is so,' Logan said, giving him a curt nod of dismissal.

Kerney stood on the top of the hotel fire-escape eyeing Main Street for any signs of Garrett. Being a tall man he could easily be spotted. What was unsettling him was the mysterious kid. Only Shorty could pick him out so he would have to be brought back to town. There was no reason for him to lie low now. The dead Plummer had implicated them all. Garrett knew who he was looking for. Without knowing the kid's likeness they would be fighting Garrett half-blinded.

By the time he had made it to the White Sands saloon, close-eyeing every alley for Garrett or suspicious-looking kids, Kerney was satisfied that Garrett, or any one associated with him, law-enforcement wise, wasn't keeping tabs on him. He was satisfied but by no means happy. Garrett gone to ground was a bigger danger than a Garrett he could see to shoot at. What game Garrett was playing by showing himself openly in Tularosa he didn't know but he sure wasn't going to have a hand in it. And he would be damned if he was going to be forced into making wrong moves by that asshole, Logan, putting pressure on him. He wasn't putting himself up to be shot at. He had underestimated what he was up against twice, costing him three men. The next time it would be Garrett and his boys who were going to shed the blood.

In the saloon he was told of Garrett coming in

and baiting them but was given a piece of positive news by Bud saying that Cass was bringing in Shorty. His stomach unkinked slightly. By what Shorty had told him the Kerney gang would outnumber Garrett's crew by two to one. Things, he felt, were swinging his way. Favouring his gang with one of his rare smiles he said, 'Boys, take it easy on the liquor. As soon as Shorty and Cass ride in we've got some barn burning to do.'

THIRTEEN

Cass and a gloomy-faced Shorty rode back along the trail to Tularosa in silence; Cass, a little to the rear of Shorty, with his hand resting on the butt of his pistol, his twitchy-eyed gaze watching Shorty in case he made a break for it. He'd had to threaten to blow Shorty's ears off to get him to leave the shack and return to Tularosa.

'I'm a dead man if the kid catches up with me,' Shorty whined when he told him the reason for the boys wanting him back in Tularosa.

'We'll all be that way if we don't know who the kid is, Shorty,' Cass said. 'So stop beefin' and get saddled up.'

'But the kid will have it in for me special like,' Shorty said. 'Not only did I steal his horse, I shot it.'

'What for?' asked Cass. 'Did it break its leg?'

'No, I just shot it,' replied Shorty. 'It seemed the right thing to do at the time being that the kid had just killed Pena and Leroy.'

Cass looked at Shorty through disbelieving eyes, as though Shorty had just related that he had cut his grandmother's throat to get at her gold teeth.

'Shorty,' he said, stone-faced, his wandering eyes rock steady. 'If you'd shot my horse out of hand even if I'd killed your pa, I'd have pegged you out, Injun-style, and lit a fire on your chest. Now get your big fat ass on to your horse or so help me I'll save the kid the price of a shell.'

'OK, Deputy,' said Garrett, 'let's go and meet them.' Both of them mounted up as they saw the dust of riders coming towards them. 'If we get the drop on them,' Garrett continued, 'we can take them in as prisoners. The fella with Shorty we can arrest on suspicion of being a cattle-thief. Shorty, we can legally hang for being a horse-thief. To save his neck he might tell us about Logan paying Kerney to kill me and Chisum. But I doubt it. I reckon Logan and Kerney kept that deal secret. Though he could finger Kerney as a rustler for us. We'll offer Kerney the same deal if it gets us Logan, when we catch him.'

As the horses pushed their way through the brush, Ben, now wearing the gunbelt again drew out both pistols and cocked them ready for action. Garrett did likewise with his Winchester. Before they came out into the clear Garrett said, 'Of course, Deputy Howard, if the sonsuvbitches are desperate foolish to want to shoot it out, don't take any chances. You just blow Shorty out of his saddle.' Garrett grinned. 'I reckon you'll want to face up to Shorty.'

Shorty and Cass came round the bend in the

trail and Shorty saw his destiny just ahead of him, the kid with two pistols fisted, pointed straight at him. His bowel-loosening panic made him do two foolish things that would send him to meet up with Pena, Leroy and Plummer: he went for his gun and jumped down from his saddle.

Ben, seeing Shorty's gun hand move downwards, fired a single shot from the Navy, a winging shot so that Garrett could have his prisoner. Shorty's jump sideways off his horse meant that the shell, instead of hitting him in the right shoulder, passed through the side of his neck, slicing the jugular in two. Shorty's lifeblood gushed out in a crimson arc, killing him before his body hit the ground in a dust-raising thud.

Cass didn't need the warmth of Shorty's blood splattering on his hands to motivate him into what action he should take. Without any hesitation, not feeling a momentary pang of sorrow and regret at not being able to avenge a *compadre*'s death, his hands shot skyward, his thinking being that Shorty had only been a chicken-livered horse-shooter who deserved to get himself plugged. With a smile as twitch-nervous as his eyes he said, 'I'm comin' in the easy way, Mr Garrett.'

Garrett, still holding his rifle steady on Cass, said, 'A wise decision, pilgrim. You can step down and unbuckle your gunbelt and sling it across here, not forgetting to do likewise with your rifle. Then you can wrap up Shorty in his blanket and put him back on his horse. Seeing that you are

Trouble on the Lordsburg Trail 131

being so friendly and co-operative me and you will have a chat on the way to Tularosa about your boss's evil ways. Like the dates he picked up cattle stolen from Mr Chisum by Billy the Kid, and what brands he changed them to, and who took them off him, possibly naming the man who hired Kerney to gun down me and Mr Chisum. If you're real forthcoming I might be able to fix it that you don't hang.' Garrett suddenly gave him a mirthless grin. 'Don't think of grabbing Shorty's gun, friend, you'd never make it. Just take it and his rifle and throw them well clear of any temptation on your part.' Garrett looked at Ben, saw the tension he was feeling by the whitening line of his jaw. 'Are you OK, Deputy?' he asked.

'Yeah, I'm OK, Mr Garrett,' Ben replied. 'It's just that I didn't mean to kill him. If he'd sat still he would have only had a busted shoulder.'

'It was Shorty's choice,' Garrett said. 'Just take it as an evening up of the score for Betsy. Come to think of it, you've got all that you took up wearing the badge for. There's nothing preventing you from continuing your journey to meet your kin.'

Ben thought for a minute or two before speaking. 'I guess Aunt Vilma will be wondering why I haven't shown up yet,' he said. 'But I don't want you to think that I'm quitting on you, there's still the rest of the Kerney gang to round up.'

'That's no problem, Mr Howard,' replied Garrett. 'If our friend here talks I'll get the local law to serve the warrants on them, that's what the sheriff of Tularosa was elected for. Logan, well, he's mine and Mr Chisum's business. So there's nothing to stop you riding on ahead to get your gear packed up and be on your way. The gang don't know you worked for me so let's keep it that way. Then none of their kin, if they want blood for blood, can track you down.' Garrett fish-eyed Cass. 'You're not thinking of causing me trouble on the trail, are you?'

Cass, busy rolling Shorty's body in his blanket, hands more bloodied from Shorty's gaping wound, gave Garrett a grimace of a smile. 'No, sir, Mr Garrett,' he said. 'That's the furthest thing from my mind.'

Garrett smiled at Ben. 'There, you see, nothing stopping you from going about your own, delayed business.' He leaned across his saddle and shook Ben's hand. 'It's been a pleasure having you as my deputy, Mr Howard. You'd make as good a lawman as your pa was, if you're *loco* enough to want to wear a badge permanently. And I'll always be beholden to you for saving mine and Mr Chisum's life. Good luck to you, wherever you finally lay down your roots.'

Ben handed Garrett his badge. 'And likewise to you, Mr Garrett, and I hope you nail Logan. Though it's been a privilege to have worn a deputy's badge it hasn't been a pleasant experience. I reckon that a man's born to be a lawman and in spite of my pa being one I must have my ma's more gentle nature in me.' Then with a final, 'So long,' he swung his horse round and headed back to Tularosa.

Trouble on the Lordsburg Trail

* * *

Ben had fed and watered his horse and was checking his saddle-straps before mounting up and setting off to complete his journey to Lordsburg. He did think of riding to the farm to let Kirsty know that he was OK. After all she had told him to look out for himself. But thinking it over again, Ben opined, Kirsty would have said that to any man who had saved her from being molested. If he'd had a stronger indication from her that she craved a closer relationship with him he might have considered paying her a visit. His pride wouldn't let him go crawling to her to seek her sweet-smiling favours.

He heard someone come into the livery barn and turning, he saw Garrett standing in the doorway, a Garrett whose hard-faced look caused his stomach to sicken with apprehension, knowing before Garrett spoke the alarming news he brought. 'It's Kirsty!' he blurted out. 'She's in trouble, isn't she!'

Garrett nodded. 'It looks that way. Sheriff Paxton told me that Kerney and his boys rode north out of town about twenty minutes ago. The farm's along that trail so your guess is as good as mine where the bastards are making for. I'm ready to ride, are you, Deputy?' And Garrett thrust the tin star in Ben's hand.

'I'm ready, Mr Garrett,' Ben said. He pinned the offered badge on to his shirt then swung up into his saddle. He was ready. Even if he was carrying a whole trunk full of diamonds for his Aunt Vilma Ben knew in which direction the greater call came from. And to hell with his pride. And Garrett noticed that there wasn't any sign of Mr Howard's ma's spoke of gentleness showing in his face.

FOURTEEN

Kirsty and Jonathan held their arms round each other for mutual comfort and strength as they watched the two, dirty-mouthing men, roughly manhandle the dining-table through the door and drop it on to the porch where more men were waiting to dump it on the wagon. Kirsty didn't know who they were, as bandannas masked the lower parts of their faces, but she guessed that they were the men with whom her stepfather had had dealings.

She had been laying the table for the evening meal when the men, three of them, came bursting into the house, giving her no time to grab for her pistol hanging on a nail by the kitchen door to defend her honour, determined not to suffer the same terrifying, degrading ordeal she had been put through by the man Mr Howard had shot. One of the men told her that if she and the boy caused no bother neither of them would be harmed.

'We've only paid you a visit to see that you quit your land,' Kerney said, satisfied by the scared looks the girl and the kid were giving him that he would have no trouble from them. Trouble, he thought, if it came, would come from outside. 'You stand there, nice and quiet-like, while my boys load up your wagon with some of your furniture. Then you haul the wagon outa here, anyways but to Tularosa. We'll be following you so if you swing back this way the kid there could have a nasty accident. And there won't be any place to come back to, I'm torching this shack once you're out of it.'

Kirsty's initial fear of being raped had faded and she was becoming more angry than frightened. She had to grip Jonathan real hard to remind herself that she was like a mother to him as well as being his sister. If anything happened to her by some foolish, futile act of defiance Jonathan would be on his own. That thought set Kirsty worrying about the well-being of Mr Howard and Mr Garrett. If these men were the men they had gone to seek out in Tularosa what had happened to them? Lying wounded, or dead, some place? Kirsty's wishful hopes of Mr Howard coming to her rescue again vanished into a deep pit of despair. Silently Kirsty began to sob and held Jonathan tighter against her.

Kerney also had worries about Garrett and the kid who was tagging along with him. He was standing on the porch watching the trail to the house, ready, if he saw any signs of movement along it, to torch the farm, the occupants still in it or not, then get to hell out of it. 'Hurry along with that loading, Bud,' he barked irritably. He didn't want to still be here when the last hour or so of

Trouble on the Lordsburg Trail 137

daylight had gone. That would give Garrett, if he showed up, the chance to Indian-up on them in the dark.

'I count six of the sonsuvbitches, Deputy Howard,' Garrett said. 'That fella on the porch I reckon must be Mr Kerney himself.'

The pair of them had dismounted behind a fold in the ground and in a crouching run; then the last few yards in a knee and elbow crawl, they went to ground in a clump of brush within 150 yards of the house.

'If we had five or six more deputies,' Garrett said, 'we could take them on man to man, and with the element of surprise on our side, win. Just the two of us could m'be down three before they bolted for cover. Then we would have a real fight on our hands, with the likelihood of the bastards slipping away as soon as it became dark.'

'If they scatter, Mr Garrett,' a sober-faced Ben said, 'They'll make for the house, could hold Kirsty and the boy hostages. Or if we fire at the house we could wound or kill them.'

Garrett had told Ben on their neck-risking ride to the farm that he had hoped that Sheriff Paxton would arrest Kerney and the members of his gang on the evidence that Cass, the man they had brought in, had freely and volubly given him to save his own skin. Paxton's telling him that Kerney and his boys had left town and the strong foreboding of where they were bound for forced him to make a quick decision. To wait for a whiskey-soak of a sheriff to round up a posse, sober enough this time of the day to m'be take part in a gun fight with noted cattle-thieves, would be wasting valuable time, putting the girl and her brother to risks he dared not think about. He had seen Cass safely locked behind bars then gone to the livery barn hoping to catch Ben before he had left for Lordsburg. Failing that, he told Ben, he would have come here on his own and done the best he could.

The look he had got back from Ben made Garrett think that his deputy would have expected no less from him. He wasn't saying it out aloud but he knew that he was blaming him and Chisum for dragging the girl into a fight she had no part in.

The pair of them watched the pieces of furniture being tossed on to the wagon, Garrett racking his brain to work out some plan that wouldn't get Kirsty and the boy hurt, and wouldn't get him and his deputy dead, leaving Kerney and his boys riding away laughing their heads off. Surprisingly, for a veteran plainsman, lawman, whatever, his greenhorn deputy came up with a plan of action first. 'We'll just have to surround them, Mr Garrett,' he heard Ben say.

Garrett cast a puzzled sidelong glance at his deputy, but could see no signs of humour in his face. 'Surround them? How?' he asked.

'There's only two men going in and out of the

house, Mr Garrett,' Ben said. 'While they're on the porch I could sneak in by the back door, get Kirsty and the boy out by the same way.' He gave Garrett a crazy-eyed grin. 'Two men, unsuspecting like, walking back inside should be no problem to a *pistolero* like myself. You can pick off those at the wagon.'

Garrett's smile was as *loco* as his deputy's. 'It isn't much of a plan but it could work, and there isn't time to think of a better one. You do it. I'll cut loose at our friends there as soon as I hear that you've started the shindig.'

Ben favoured Garrett with another glory-boy grin then slipped from his side. Garrett slowly shook his head. He was definitely getting too old to be riding alongside young hellions. He pumped a shell into the chamber of the Winchester, brought it up to his shoulder and drew a bead on the man standing in the wagon.

Kirsty, casting hateful looks at the two men carrying out what pieces of furniture that took their fancy, felt Jonathan tugging at the sleeve of her dress. She glanced down at him.

'Sis,' he whispered, and nodded towards the kitchen door.

Kirsty's heart gave a wild leap. Mr Howard was standing in the kitchen. It took all her willpower for her not to show the immense relief and happiness in her face at seeing him unhurt and having come back to help her and Jonathan.

Ben took a quick look into the living-room and saw the two men step on to the porch and move out of his line of sight. He waved for Kirsty and Jonathan to come and join him as he kept a watchful eye, and a steady gun on the porch door. Kirsty could see that the men still had their backs to her. Hardly daring to breathe she grabbed hold of Jonathan's hand and ran, light-footed into the kitchen.

'Outside, quickly!' Ben said softly but urgently. 'Keep well clear of the house. Go now!'

Kirsty gave his arm a squeeze and as uninhibited as though she had done it many times before, kissed Ben full on the lips. Then she and Jonathan ran out of the house. As it happened Ben had a few seconds in which to savour the sweetness of the kiss.

'That's enough loading, Bud,' Kerney said irritably. 'It's time we were long gone. You get the torch lit, Sam, bring that bucket of coal oil, and let's get this place burnin'.' Raising his voice he shouted, 'You in the shack there! You've got a coupla minutes to get what you want to save before we put a torch to the place!'

Ben's dreamy-eyed look vanished. He stepped out of the kitchen and aimed both pistols at the front door, trying not to think that his first kiss from Kirsty could also be his last one. He gritted his teeth. One thing was for sure the kissing days, or any other days, of the two bastards who were about to walk through that door were all but over.

Bud came in off the porch holding a spluttering, smoky, dried-brushwood torch, stopping suddenly in the doorway at the unexpected change in the

Trouble on the Lordsburg Trail 141

room. Where the girl and the boy had been standing there now was a fierce-faced youth holding two big pistols on him. His brain had hardly time to register the changed scenario, and to do something about it, when Ben's two slugs hit him full in the chest, ending his thinking processes for eternity. The smashing impact of the point-blank range shots threw Bud back against Sam. Sam stumbled sideways, cursing as the coal oil splashed over his arms.

As Bud fell to the floor the torch, slipping from lifeless fingers, dropped into the bucket. Searing flames flared up in front of Sam, setting his clothes and hair alight. An agonizing screaming Sam flung the flaming bucket away and leapt off the porch wildly flailing his arms to beat out the flames.

Ben walked to the door and, more out of compassion than anger, shot Sam in the back of the head. Sam fell flat on his face in the dirt with the flames he could no longer feel eating at his flesh still licking about his body.

'Jesus,' breathed a more than slightly shaken Garrett. His deputy had certainly started the ball with a spectacular opening number. Kerney and the rest of the gang stood as though carved from wood for a few horrified minutes at the sight of the human fireball, presenting Garrett with easy targets. He shot the man he had drawn a bead on, and one of his *compadres*, dead with two quick shots.

Ben, hearing Garrett's rifle coming into action,

stepped out on to the porch and began firing single-spaced shots at Kerney and the only man left on his feet at the wagon. Kerney jumped down from the porch and flung himself behind the wagon tailgate. The other man stood his ground blazing away at Ben. Ben brought both pistols on him and he fell against a wheel to die quickly but noisily from two stomach wounds.

If Kerney had had a soul or been blessed with sensitive feelings he would have cried at seeing his gang destroyed in a matter of minutes. Shorty had warned him that the kid was good. He had just bitterly learned how right Shorty had been. He poked his pistol round the side of the wagon to get a clear shot at the kid the moment the son-of-a-bitch had emptied his pistols. In his eagerness to down Ben, Kerney forgot about Garrett. The shifting of his body gave Garrett a sighting of his right leg, all an expert shot with a rifle like Garrett, needed. Kerney howled like a viciously kicked dog and rolled clear of the wagon, clutching at his shattered knee with both hands.

Ben strode to the edge of the porch and looked across at the rear of the wagon. Keeping his pistols on the writhing, loudly moaning Kerney he rightly concluded that he was in too much pain to try a sneaky shot at him and put them away.

'It's all over, Mr Garrett,' he called out, but Garrett was already running in to join him.

Holding hands, Kirsty and Jonathan stepped on to the far end of the porch. Ben turned. 'Better go inside,' he said. 'These are sights a girl and a young boy shouldn't see.'

'I'd be obliged if you could heat some water, and some cloths for bandages, Miss Kirsty,' Garrett said. 'So I can patch this fella up for the trip to Tularosa.'

'I'll do that, Mr Garrett,' replied Kirsty, and dragged a reluctant, goggle-eyed Jonathan into the house with her.

Kerney began to puncture his groans with obscenities. 'Stop that kind of talk,' Ben said, 'or I'll bend the barrel of my Navy over your head.'

'You'd better do as he says, Kerney,' a grinning Garrett told him. 'You can see by what's just happened here he's a mean sonuvabitch when roused.' He stooped and picked up Kerney and carried him indoors.

Kerney's leg had been bandaged up and the bleeding stopped and Garrett thought that he would be able to make the trip to town without losing any more blood. He hadn't finished with Kerney yet. He needed to talk long and revealing, as Cass had done.

'Me and Mr Howard will put your furniture back, Miss Kirsty,' he said. 'Then I'd like to borrow the wagon to take the dead back to Tularosa. You can keep their horses and saddle gear, they'll be worth a tidy sum. They owe you something for all the upset they've caused you. I'll sign a bill of sale for them so it will all be legal and above board.' Garrett smiled fatherly at Kirsty. 'You'll get no more trouble from anyone, I guarantee it. That's if you still want to stay. Though I'll admit you've had enough trouble these past few days to make you want to pull up stakes. But as I said, those days are over.'

'I'm staying, Mr Garrett,' Kirsty said firmly. 'It's mine and Jonathan's land and we intend to work it. I was thinking of selling up but not any more.' Bold-eyeing Ben she said, 'Will your business fetch you this way again, Mr Howard?'

Kirsty prayed that it would. That was the only reason she was staying on the farm. Then there would be no excuse for him not to come back to call on her, if he wanted to. If she sold up and moved out he would get the impression that she didn't want to see him again. And unless Mr Howard was as fond of her as she was of him he wouldn't bother to seek her out at her new home.

Ben wanted to tell Kirsty that he wished he could stay right now but family ties and deathbed wishes had to be honoured first. Instead he said, 'I don't rightly know what arrangements my kin have made for me in Lordsburg, Miss Kirsty.' Then eyeing her just as directly he added, 'If I can, I intend coming back to Tularosa. It's as good a place as any to look for work.'

And Kirsty had to leave it at that. She had asked, albeit not as Jonathan had wanted her to by coming out and entreating Mr Howard to stay. But she reckoned that she had gone more than halfway, feeling that Mr Howard knew that it hadn't been just a question she had just said but a deep-felt plea.

* * *

Garrett halted the wagon close by a small stand of cottonwoods. 'This looks a likely place, Deputy Howard,' he said. 'Light the lantern so that we can see that the rope is tightly knotted.'

Kerney, feeling that it wouldn't be long before he met up with his boys again, their wrapped-up bodies, jostling and bumping up against him with the movement of the wagon, stopped his groaning. 'Rope! What the hell are you talkin' about?' he said, fear rising in his voice.

'We're talking about hanging you, Kerney,' Garrett said. 'That's why I didn't kill you right off. My deputy here has never witnessed a hanging and he opines that you'll make a good first one for him, being that you sicced your man, Plummer, on to his girl.'

'Hang me! Hang me!' Kerney's voice was a frightened girl's hysterical shriek and in spite of his painful wound he sat bolt upright on the wagon bed in his panic. 'You murderin' sonuvabitch, you can't do that, it ain't lawful!'

'Now, now, Mr Kerney,' chided Garrett. 'Since when have you been concerned about things being lawful? You haven't done a lawful act since you were big enough to wear a gun.' Garrett got up from the seat. 'You bring the rope and the lantern, I'll bring Mr Kerney along.'

Kerney cursed then screamed with pain as Garrett lifted him up.

'That isn't fitting language for a man to use,'

Garrett told him. 'Not when he's about to meet his Maker in a few minutes time.'

Entering into the spirit of putting the fear of God into Kerney, Ben snarled, 'Stop the sweet-talking, Mr Garrett, let's get the bastard dancing under one of those trees. Then we go and get his boss, Logan, and do the same to him.'

'That isn't going to be easy, Deputy,' Garrett said, holding on to the still struggling Kerney. 'Logan's a big man hereabouts and while Cass has given us proof that Logan's up to his neck in the cattle-lifting trade we haven't got proof that he paid the fella we're about to string up to kill me and Mr Chisum.'

'I'll give you proof, Mr Garrett,' Kerney cried, clutching desperately at a possible straw in the gale of misfortune that was hitting him. 'I swear, on my mother's grave, I'll give you proof enough to put him inside! If you give me your word not to string me up.'

'What do you think, Deputy?' Garrett said. 'Logan's the bigger fish.'

Ben gave Kerney a hard-eyed look. 'Hang the sonuvabitch I say, Mr Garrett, but you're the man in charge, it's your decision.'

Garrett let Kerney sweat it out for a few minutes before he spoke again. 'Are you prepared to sign a paper to that effect, Mr Kerney? You're not bluffing me to try and save your neck? If you are you're only grabbing yourself a short space of time. You can see that my deputy will be upset if I don't hang you and as sure as hell he won't let me give you a second chance if you're only stalling.'

'Yes damnit! I'll sign!' Kerney cried. 'I'll put my name to a whole sheaf of papers as long as you don't go back on your word, and get me to a doc so that I can get my leg seen to before it turns bad on me!'

'Good,' said Garrett, winking at Ben as he lowered Kerney back on to the bed of the wagon. 'I'll put in a good word for you to the judge, telling him you've been helpful and you'll only do time like your buddy, Cass.' He sat down and jerked at the reins and the wagon rolled forward, Kerney letting out an extra loud moaning scream every time the wagon hit a rut in the trail.

Ben and Garrett were standing outside the sheriff's office. The wagon had been unloaded of its grisly load, Sheriff Paxton wondering if Garrett was in partnership with the undertaker the number of customers he was bringing him in, had told them that he would see that the wagon was returned to the farm. Kerney, after signing an affidavit implicating Logan as the man behind the attack on Chisum, had had his wound attended to professionally, and was now, as Garrett had promised, sharing a cell with Cass.

'I intend serving the warrant on Logan myself, Mr Howard,' Garrett said. 'So you can hand in your badge, again.' Garrett smiled. 'And be on your way to Lordsburg for real this time.'

'Isn't that risky, Mr Garrett?' Ben said. 'I thought you said Logan had a tough crew.'

'He has,' replied Garrett. 'If I was to ride on to his home range with a whole passel of deputies in no time at all there would be lead flying around. Logan's excuse would be that his crew thought that they were firing on a bunch of border cattle-lifters. And he would get away with it. The law isn't a cut-and-dried process in this part of the woods, Mr Howard. On my own I might just be able to sweet-talk my way into the big house.'

'I'd like to ride with you,' Ben said. 'I've still got a stake in this game, Mr Garrett. Logan made it my business from the beginning when Kerney's boys were going to plug me at your camp. And meaning no disrespect, you need help. Even my pa wouldn't have been so *loco* to try what you are going to do on your own. Unless you've got some special reason for me not to do so I'd like to hang on to my badge for another day.'

'Deputy Howard,' replied Garrett, 'the only reason I didn't want you to ride with me was because if you got yourself shot a girl not a million miles from here would put a load of buckshot in my ass.' Garrett narrow-eyed Ben. 'Have you taken your possible future with Miss Kirsty into consideration? I know the pair of you haven't publicly declared your undying love for each other but even a hard-hearted son-of-a-bitch like me can see how favourable you feel towards each other.'

Ben coloured up. 'M'be I have strong feelings towards Miss Kirsty, how she feels towards me I don't rightly know. All I know is that you promised her that she would never be bothered again. What if things go wrong for you, and Logan's still the big stompin' man around here? Will he not still want to get his dirty hands on her land?' Ben gimlet-eyed Garrett. 'What price then the promise you made to her that she would never have to face that kind of trouble again, Mr Garrett?'

'Damn all, Deputy,' Garrett admitted soberly. 'Keep the badge, I'd be pleased to have you come along with me. I just didn't think I'd the right to ask you.' He grinned. 'Now we know how we stand with each other I suggest we get a few hours' sleep in, tomorrow could turn out to be a heavy day for us.'

FIFTEEN

'We must be on the Bar X home range now, Deputy,' said Garrett as they dropped down into a wide, grassy, well-watered depression in the broad arid plain some two hours' ride from Tularosa.

Beyond the bunches of grazing longhorns Ben suddenly saw the dust spirals of fast moving riders and stiffened up in his saddle. 'Company closing in on us, Mr Garrett,' he said.

'I see 'em,' replied Garrett, and eased his Winchester out of its boot. He thin-smiled Ben. 'I'm not starting to worry yet but it don't make sense not to be prepared for the worst. A fella could live longer thinking that way.'

Ben, also thinking along those lines, loosened his coat so that he had freer access to the Navy. Both pulled up their mounts and waited for the riders to close in on them. Both giving each other confident grins that didn't reflect their true inner feelings and hopes.

'The hatchet-faced *hombre* in front is Spicer, Logan's straw boss,' Garrett said, as the four riders drew up in a rough semicircle around them.

Spicer gave Garrett a surprised look.

'You're a long ways off your rounds, Garrett,' he said. 'Chisum's law don't reach this far south.'

'I'm holding a warrant for your boss's arrest, Spicer,' Garrett said.

Spicer burst out laughing. 'I'll say this for you, Garrett, you've got balls.' He cast a disparaging look at Ben. 'And you'll need them and then some, lookin' at the help you've brung along.'

'Don't underestimate the kid, Spicer,' Garrett said. 'He practically wiped out the Kerney gang on his own. I reckon you've heard of Kerney, Spicer. Made Billy the Kid and his wild boys back down too. Now whatever else you boys think I am, I'm no liar. The kid's good. But I'm hoping he don't have to prove it.'

Spicer's face slowly began to lose its cocksure look. The boring-eyed glare the kid was favouring him with made him think that Garrett was telling the truth. Garrett wasn't a fool. He wouldn't have come on Bar X land without a good man to back him up.

'If I wanted a war,' Garrett continued, 'I would have come prepared for one. All I want is you to let me and my deputy through to the big house to serve this warrant on Logan for being the instigator in a plot to kill Mr Chisum.'

Spicer's gaze swivelled on to Garrett. 'Kill old man Chisum?' he gasped, doubting Garrett's words.

Garrett nodded. 'I've Kerney's signed confession to prove it, Spicer. I know that Chisum is a hard man but that don't warrant him being killed. Why if all the hard men in the territory deserved to be dead there'd only be the babes in arms left in the State.'

The rider to the left of Spicer, an elderly, leather-faced man said, 'I rode for the Jingle Bob outfit for a spell, Spicer, and as Garrett said Chisum was a hard man, but he treats his crew fair, paid us top money. If Logan's been hiring bushwhackers to gun down Chisum then I ain't willin' to pull out my hogleg to stop Garrett servin' his piece of paper.'

Behind him Spicer heard the rumble of muttered support for the sentiments expressed. He took another assaying glance at Ben to see if there was just an outside chance of taking him on and winning through. There wasn't, he quickly concluded, not when it looked as though he had lost the backing of his boys. And Logan's willingness to see Chisum killed rubbed him on the raw as well, making him doubt his loyalty to his boss. With a growled, 'Come on boys, let's go and check on those beeves at the water-hole. This ain't any of our business,' he jerked his horse's head round, and with hooves kicking up the dust they rode past Ben and Garrett.

Garrett heaved a loud sigh of relief at their going. 'That's the hardest part over and I got myself worried for nothing. Now let's go and beard Logan in his den.'

Logan watched them ride in through the window of his house, recognizing the tall figure of

Trouble on the Lordsburg Trail 153

Garrett. He knew, as if Garrett had sent him a wire, why he was riding up to his front door. Kerney must have talked. But why hadn't Spicer, or any of his crew, stopped Garrett? Brought him here to the big house under escort, or lying dead across his horse? Logan felt fear's cold fingers clawing at his stomach.

He opened the door and shouted, 'Felipe, here, quickly!' The Mexican who bossed the household peons answered his call. 'There's two men about to call on me,' Logan told him. 'When you show them in here you go out to the porch and watch what's going on inside. If I pull my handkerchief out and wipe my face you shoot both of them dead, the tall *hombre* first, savvy?'

'*Si patron*,' replied Felipe without asking why, the *patron's* word being the law on the hacienda.

Garrett and Ben dismounted and walked under the coolness of a shingle-roofed porch. The Mexican who opened one side of the big wooden, iron-studded door in answer to Garrett's knocking, indicated by the inclining of his head that they were to come inside. Still shut-mouthed he led them along a stone paved passage to a door at the far end of it. He knocked on it and a growled, 'Enter!' sounded from inside the room. And Ben saw for the first time the man who had hired the no-good scum to force Miss Kirsty off her land. A bulky, florid-faced man sitting in a big leather chair behind a desk larger than the room he had slept in at home. A big man who fitted the grand style of his big house.

Ben didn't give him a second glance. The dead-eyed look the silent-tongued Mexican had given him and Garrett as he closed the door set alarm signals twanging in his brain. An alarm system that Ben didn't know he possessed. He could only think that they had been passed on to him by his pa when born. Only half-listening to Garrett telling Logan the reason for his visit he kept his eyes and ears on the door leading into the room and the double glass doors that led on to the porch, the danger spots.

'You'll never make the charge stick, Garrett,' Logan said. 'My word against a man like Kerney? You'll be laughed out of court.'

'M'be so,' Garrett said. 'But mud sticks and I'll see that it sticks real hard. Hard enough for your political friends up at the State capital to deny that they ever even knew you. Your reaching-high days will be over for good, Logan.'

Logan had fought hard and dirty to get where he was and he would fight harder and dirtier to stay there. He had known all along that Garrett was the biggest threat to achieving his ambition. No other lawman would act on a statement made by a thieving asshole like Kerney. Garrett's time for dying was right here and now. 'You take me to court, Garrett, and I'll sue you for wrongful arrest. I'll break you.' Casually his hand moved to the top pocket of his coat and pulling out a fine white silk handkerchief he dabbed at his brow with it.

Out of the corner of his eye Ben caught a slight blurring of the light coming through the glass porch doors. His alarm signals rang like the bells of hell in his ears. He pivoted round on one leg, Colt fisted, and triggered off two shots at the part figure he could now clearly see. The shattering of glass echoed the sound of the shots as Felipe fell headlong into the room, dead from two closely spaced bullet holes in his head. His pistol slid across the highly polished floor, coming to a stop against a leg of Logan's chair. Logan's lifelong philosophy of planning at least two moves ahead went by the board. Blinded by rage that Garrett had survived a second attempt to kill him he grabbed for the pistol to do the job himself. Garrett's single shot smashed into his shoulder before his fingers touched the pistol, flinging him groaning with pain hard up against the back of his chair, with his mind in shock, not yet fully realizing what had happened to him.

Ben peered both ways along the porch through the broken door. 'There seems to be no more of them skulkin' around, Mr Garrett,' he said, and slipped his pistol back into the waistband of his pants.

'Thanks to your quick eye, Deputy, I wasn't caught short,' Garrett said gratefully. 'I ought to have known the sonuvabitch wouldn't give up all he has without some sort of a fight.' He looked dispassionately at the semi-conscious Logan, blood-drained-faced, slumped back in his chair. 'One thing's for sure, he's played his last trick, for what good it did for him. And you, Mr Howard, have finished being a deputy from right now.' He grinned. 'No offence intended.'

'What about him?' Ben nodded at Logan, surprised at the abruptness of Garrett's dismissal of his services.

'I think he's passed causing me any bother, Mr Howard,' replied Garrett. 'I'll get him to Tularosa OK. But I want you ass-kicking it off Bar X range but fast. Some of the crew will be riding up to the big house soon to find out what the shooting was about. They may have heard from Spicer, or the boys who were with him, that a genuine *pistolero* is here. The young bucks who fancy themselves as fast-draw men could call you out to prove it and you could find yourself having to do a heap of unnecessary shooting. That activity wouldn't please Miss Kirsty, would it now?'

'It sure wouldn't make me happy either, Mr Garrett,' Ben said. 'If I'd known that when I crossed the Pegos I would end up doing all this killing I would have stayed at home and mailed my ma's jewellery on to Aunt Vilma.'

'You didn't kill anyone who wasn't trying to do likewise to you, Mr Howard,' Garrett said. He grinned. 'Looking on the positive side, if you hadn't come across the Pegos you would never have met up with Miss Kirsty. Now go and get on your way to Lordsburg or you may never get there; we've already said our goodbyes. You can keep the badge, give it to your first boy. Tell him how you earned it, if it won't keep him awake at night.'

'I only hope it don't keep me awake at night, Mr

Garrett,' a sober-faced Ben said. 'It ain't what you call an easy-on-the-nerves job being a lawman, that's for sure.' Ben took a final look at Logan and the dead Mexican and left Garrett walking round the desk to tend to Logan.

Ben's Aunt Vilma looked at the jewellery Ben had spread out on the table with tear-moistened eyes. 'It was good of you to come all this way to bring them to me. It was a promise your mother and me made when we were young girls, before we even had as much as a string of glass beads between us. I only wish that you hadn't had to make the trip. I hope you had no trouble getting here, Ben, we heard that there is a war going on up in Lincoln County. You certainly look as though you need a few days' rest, and a good feeding up.'

'It's been no trouble at all, Aunt Vilma,' said Ben, with the smooth-face and unblinking eyes of a natural born liar.

'I'm surprised you haven't got a steady girl, Ben,' his aunt said, 'with high hopes of marrying her. Then you could have kept the jewellery for her.' When Ben didn't answer her straight away she close-eyed him then smiled. 'There is a girl, Ben, isn't there?' she asked softly.

'Yes there is, Aunt Vilma,' Ben replied. 'Well, sort of I reckon. I met her in Tularosa; she's called Kirsty.'

'A fine name, Kirsty,' Aunt Vilma said and gave her nephew a womanly understanding look. 'You'll not be figuring to stay here in Lordsburg with me and your Uncle Joe, will you? Well not after the few days it will take me to put some flesh back on your bones.'

'If it's not putting you and Uncle Joe out by me not staying with you, I would like to ride back to Tularosa,' an eager-eyed Ben said.

Aunt Vilma laughed. 'Of course it isn't putting us out. We only offered you a place here if you had no place else to go. You've got your own life to live. Now you stay with us for three or four days then get yourself back to that Kirsty you think you have.' Aunt Vilma wrapped the pieces of jewellery back in the cloth again and pushed it across the table to Ben. Smiling, she said, 'Give them to your future wife, tell her they're a wedding present from her new aunt.' Aunt Vilma saw that Ben was going to protest and stopped him by raising a hand. 'It's what your mother would have wanted, Ben; so that's the end of the matter. Now get yourself out back and get washed, there'll be food on the table when you come back in.'

Kirsty heard Jonathan's excited shout of, 'Mr Howard's ridin' in, Sis!' and rushed out to the porch, thankful that she had kept wearing her dresses in the hope that such a day like this would happen.

Jonathan grinned up at Ben as he drew up his mount alongside the porch. 'You've come back, Mr Howard,' he said.

A po-faced Ben said, 'I had to, Jonathan. Your sister promised to mend this hole in my coat.' He poked his finger through the bullet hole. 'And she ain't done so.'

Equally straight-faced Kirsty said, 'I never did, Ben, did I? But if you care to step down and come on inside I'll fix it right away.'

'There's no rush, Kirsty,' Ben said. 'I intend staying hereabouts for quite a spell.' Smiling broadly he dismounted.